Acting Edition

Peter Pan and Wendy: A New Old Adventure

by Lauren M. Gunderson

Adapted from the Play by
J. M. Barrie

Copyright © 2024 by Lauren M. Gunderson
All Rights Reserved

PETER PAN AND WENDY is fully protected under the copyright laws of the United States of America, the British Commonwealth, including Canada, and all member countries of the Berne Convention for the Protection of Literary and Artistic Works, the Universal Copyright Convention, and/or the World Trade Organization conforming to the Agreement on Trade Related Aspects of Intellectual Property Rights. All rights, including professional and amateur stage productions, recitation, lecturing, public reading, motion picture, radio broadcasting, television, online/digital production, and the rights of translation into foreign languages are strictly reserved.

ISBN 978-0-573-71087-2

www.concordtheatricals.com
www.concordtheatricals.co.uk

FOR PRODUCTION INQUIRIES

UNITED STATES AND CANADA
info@concordtheatricals.com
1-866-979-0447

UNITED KINGDOM AND EUROPE
licensing@concordtheatricals.co.uk
020-7054-7298

Each title is subject to availability from Concord Theatricals Corp., depending upon country of performance. Please be aware that *PETER PAN AND WENDY* may not be licensed by Concord Theatricals Corp. in your territory. Professional and amateur producers should contact the nearest Concord Theatricals Corp. office or licensing partner to verify availability.

CAUTION: Professional and amateur producers are hereby warned that *PETER PAN AND WENDY* is subject to a licensing fee. The purchase, renting, lending or use of this book does not constitute a license to perform this title(s), which license must be obtained from Concord Theatricals Corp. prior to any performance. Performance of this title(s) without a license is a violation of federal law and may subject the producer and/or presenter of such performances to civil penalties. Both amateurs and professionals considering a production are strongly advised to apply to the appropriate agent before starting rehearsals, advertising, or booking a theatre. A licensing fee must be paid whether the title(s) is presented for charity or gain and whether or not admission is charged. Professional/Stock licensing fees are quoted upon application to Concord Theatricals Corp.

This work is published by Samuel French, an imprint of Concord Theatricals Corp.

No one shall make any changes in this title(s) for the purpose of production. No part of this book may be reproduced, stored in a retrieval system, scanned, uploaded, or transmitted in any form, by any means, now known or yet to be invented, including mechanical, electronic, digital, photocopying, recording, videotaping, or otherwise, without the prior written permission of the publisher. No one shall share this title(s), or any part of this title(s), through any social media or file hosting websites.

For all inquiries regarding motion picture, television, online/digital and other media rights, please contact Concord Theatricals Corp.

MUSIC AND THIRD-PARTY MATERIALS USE NOTE

Licensees are solely responsible for obtaining formal written permission from copyright owners to use copyrighted music and/or other copyrighted third-party materials (e.g. artworks, logos) in the performance of this play and are strongly cautioned to do so. If no such permission is obtained by the licensee, then the licensee must use only original music and materials that the licensee owns and controls. Licensees are solely responsible and liable for clearances of all third-party copyrighted materials, including without limitation music, and shall indemnify the copyright owners of the play(s) and their licensing agent, Concord Theatricals Corp., against any costs, expenses, losses and liabilities arising from the use of such copyrighted third-party materials by licensees. For music, please contact the appropriate music licensing authority in your territory for the rights to any incidental music.

IMPORTANT BILLING AND CREDIT REQUIREMENTS

If you have obtained performance rights to this title, please refer to your licensing agreement for important billing and credit requirements.

PETER PAN AND WENDY was commissioned by Shakespeare Theatre Company and received its world premiere at Harman Hall in Washington, DC, on December 9, 2019, under Artistic Director Simon Godwin and Executive Director Chris Jennings. The production was directed by Alan Paul with original music by Jenny Giering, sets by Jason Sherwood, costumes by Loren Shaw, lighting by Isabella Byrd, sound by John Gromada, projections by Jared Mezzocchi, puppets by James Ortiz, flying sequence choreography by Paul Rubin, fight choreography by David Leong, choreography by Katie Spelman, animal coordination by William Berloni, and special effects by Jeremy Chernick. The production was stage managed by Joseph Smelser. The cast was as follows:

WENDY DARLING . . . . Sinclair Daniel
MRS. DARLING/TINKERBELL . . . . Jenni Barber
JOHN DARLING . . . . Christopher Flaim
MICHAEL DARLING . . . . Chauncey Chestnut
MR. DARLING/CAPTAIN HOOK . . . . Derek Smith
PETER PAN . . . . Justin Mark
TIGER LILY . . . . Isabella Star LaBlanc
TOOTLES . . . . Francisco González
CURLY . . . . Ronen Lewis
SLIGHTLY . . . . .Joriah Kwame
TWINS . . . . Darren Alford, Tendo Nsubuga
SMEE . . . . Tom Story
STARKEY . . . . Gregory Wooddell
JUKES . . . . Michael Glenn
NOODLER . . . . Calvin McCullough
ENSEMBLE . . . . Oliver Archibald, Megan Huynh,
                                                      Joseph Respicio
UNDERSTUDIES . . . . Angeleaza Anderson, Damondre Green,
                                                      Malcolm Fuller
NANA . . . . Bailey (trained by William Berloni)

CHARACTERS

Real World: All British

WENDY DARLING – fourteen, precocious, smart, ambitious girl
MRS. DARLING – her mother, kind but hurried
   (Can double as **TINKERBELL)**
JOHN DARLING – twelve, middle son, anxious
MICHAEL DARLING – nine, youngest son, adventurous
MR. DARLING – their father, pompous and unthinking
   (Can double as **CAPTAIN HOOK**)
NANA – the family dog

Neverland:

PETER PAN – both fifteen and ageless, a rebellious, confident, excitable boy, also American.
TINKERBELL – a spunky fairy with mean girl vibes
TIGER LILY – fifteen, proud, smart, wisecracking Indigenous girl
TOOTLES – Lost Boy
CURLY – Lost Boy
SLIGHTLY – Lost Boy
SHADOW – Peter's mischievous shadow
JEROME THE CROCODILE – a very large crocodile with a clock in its belly

Pirates:

CAPTAIN HOOK – the one and only, mean, strong, determined
SMEE – Pirate, his second in command and a certifiable "yes man"
STARKEY – Pirate
JUKES – Pirate
NOODLER – Pirate

Casting Note
Lost Boys and Pirates can be played by any gender.

SETTING

Edwardian London, The Sky, Neverland.

TIME

1903 and Always.

AUTHOR'S NOTES

Formatting Notes

Lines that are **bolded** should be the lines that are most clearly heard in synchronous dialogue.

Lines that end with en dashes (–) are meant to be cut off by the subsequent line.

Lines that end in (or include) ellipses (...) indicate hesitation. The speaker doesn't know what or how to say what they need to say next. Please don't adlib, rather embrace the pause.

Stair
> **Step**
>> **Lines** are to indicate fast cue pick up and slight overlap.

Character Note

Nana has been successfully played by a live dog as well as a puppet. Peter's Shadow has been successfully portrayed as a digital or real shadow as well as an actor (or two). Jerome is an opportunity for great puppetry or other special effects. Tinkerbell's Fairy Friends in Act Two have been successfully produced as toy glow balls manipulated by the ensemble. You are welcome to add a non-speaking mermaid to the top of Act Two if you like: one was beautifully accomplished before and was quite magical and memorable.

A Note on Tiger Lily's Music

When producing *Peter Pan and Wendy*, productions should be careful not to use actual Indigenous songs as they are deeply significant to their particular tribes and should not be repurposed.

A DEEP THANK YOU

To our Indigenous cultural consultants Anthony Hudson and Anonymous, as well as our actor Isabella Star LeBlanc who premiered the role of Tiger Lily.

Thank you to Kansas City Repertory Theatre under the leadership of Artistic Director Stuart Carden for the finishing commission and for the beautiful second production.

THE MYTH OF NEVERLAND

In my reimagining of the Peter Pan myth, Neverland has been born entirely from Peter Pan himself. When Peter was a very small boy in the very real world, he heard his first story about a mystical world of fairies and magical creatures, heroes and villains, adventure and triumph. Young Peter decided in that very moment that he wanted to live where the story never stops, nor the characters ever grow up. He wanted to live *in* a story of his own. And so he did. The fairy, Tinkerbell, appeared from his imagination and took him toward the second star to the right and straight on till morning, and Peter found himself in Neverland, a perfect world for a little boy's dreams of fearless valor. But little boys are restless and quickly bored, so Peter continued to add to Neverland by flying back to the real world of Edwardian England, listening to any story he could, and bringing back parts of those stories he most enjoyed in order to continue growing his perfect fantastical wonderland.

Of course, what Peter doesn't know he's doing is only bringing back the stories that interest *him*, the ones that make *him* the hero, the one where heroism looks and acts one particular way. Like anyone on earth who listens to only one kind of story, that means that lots of other stories and lots of other kinds of heroes are left out. Is Neverland a place for everyone, or just for Peter Pan? This is the lesson Peter will learn in the play you're about to read...

REACTIONARY DIALOGUE FOR PIRATES AND KIDS TO USE DURING FIGHTS

To fill in the world of the play, ensemble members should not be quiet, but rather can employ any of the following phrases or exclamations when Peter and Hook are battling. We don't want a silent fight now do we. Enjoy!

KIDS.

*(To cheer on **PETER**.)*
Keep on him, Peter!

Get him, Pan!
Show him Peter! Shut him up!
Watch out! Look out! Look up!

At your back/side/top!
He's coming back!
Duck! Strike! You can do it!
GoGoGo! He's coming for you!
Move! Hurry! Fly! Run!
Get out of the way!
Look behind you!
Hit him again!
Watch your back!
Watch your sword!
Nonono! He's still up!
Be careful, Peter!
Take him down, Peter!

PIRATES.

*(To cheer on **HOOK**.)*
Straight through the heart, Captain!

Gut him! Slice him up!
Strike him down!
Blow the man down!
(*i.e. Kill him!*)

Blimey, Captain!
Slay him, Buccaneer!
Come about, Captain!
You got him now!
Show him the steel!
Take the boy out!
On your left/right/back!
A palpable hit, Captain!
End them all! Send 'em!

(To antagonize **HOOK** *or* **PIRATES**.*)*	*(To antagonize* **LOST BOYS**.*)*
Back off Hook! Back off, you big oaf!	Come here, you little twit!
You dumb pirate!	You little ninny!
You bigheaded ass!	You lily-livered rascal!
KIDS.	**PIRATES**.
You're not so tough/stong/scary/big!	You stupid little rat!
Peter'll beat you like he always does!	Get lost, Lost Boy!
You can't stop Pan/us!	Avast there, you scourge!
No one can stop us!	Fight like a man!
Think you're faster than us?	Stand still! Give up!
Get ready to lose!	Shut up!
Can't catch me!	You can do better than that.
	Try again, you whiny brat!
	Why don't you just die!
	We'll send you to the deep!

ACT ONE

Scene One

The Nursery

*(This is the same Edwardian nursery you're expecting. Three beds for three kids. Toys and books all over the room. Chests of drawers, armoire, book cases, lamps of all sizes. A large bay window is open with a breeze tossing the curtains by our **WENDY**, who looks through a small telescope at the night sky.)*

*(**WENDY** is in her nightgown and sweater but is studious in her astronomy.)*

(Suddenly she sees something in the night sky and stops.)

WENDY. What on earth is that? Or to be more accurate, what in the northwest quadrant of the celestial sphere is that?

(She gets out her astronomy book to consult.)

Yes, that star is most certainly out of place. Which begs the question: Do stars get lost? Hm. I suppose everyone does at some point in their lives. And stars have very long lives. Perhaps I should alert the Royal Society to the fact that all of astronomy is now in question –

(*But while her back was turned a small* **BALL OF LIGHT** *[otherwise known as* **TINKERBELL***] has rushed into the nursery through the window and hid in a drawer.*)

(**WENDY** *hears the drawer slam and looks around the room but sees nothing. Then she looks back through the telescope. The stray star is gone.*)

WENDY. Well look at that. The star must've righted itself. What a well-behaved ball of gas. Astronomy is safe again I suppose. Goodnight then, stars. The well-behaved ones and the mischievous.

(**WENDY** *goes to close the window when the drawer rattles to stop her.* **WENDY** *stops. Then closes the window – the draw rattles –* **WENDY** *stops.*)

(**WENDY** *goes to the drawer and opens it, hesitant, curious… The* **BALL OF LIGHT** *flies out of the drawer and to the window, trying to get out like a trapped fly.*)

OH MY WORD! What is this? What are you?! Some tiny sun in my room that – OW – pinches!? Get out! Out! What is happening? This is quite incorrect astronomy!

(*The* **BALL OF LIGHT** *flies around the room angrily until* **WENDY** *traps it in the armoire just as…*)

(*Her mother,* **MRS. DARLING** *enters. Of course* **WENDY** *is now in a disheveled state and* **MRS. DARLING** *goes right to primping her.*)

MRS. DARLING. Wendy Wendy Wendy, what is this fuss?

WENDY. A light, Mother! There's a light in my room.

MRS. DARLING. Well yes, there are several. Why are you not in bed?

WENDY. No a *ball* of light! A little star! And it flew around with such haste!

MRS. DARLING. Then it must've been late for something. *(Calling out.)* Boys! *(To* **WENDY**.*)* Why must you look so very mussed come bedtime. It's neither good for the hair, nor the face, nor the stress of your mother. *Boys!*

WENDY. I'm mussed because I was chasing a ball of pinchy light around the room!

MRS. DARLING. *Wendy.* These stories are not a welcome amusement for a girl your age. We must begin to turn you into a lady, and ladies do not miss their bedtimes, nor stare at the stars all night, nor engage in such childish nonsense.

  WENDY. But Mother –

    MRS. DARLING. Which is why you'll be moving to your own room next week.

      WENDY. What?

        MRS. DARLING. Wendy –

          WENDY. A *new* room. But this *is* my room. I'm the eldest, I was here first.

MRS. DARLING. And you must be the first to grow up. I've prepared a beautiful place for you upstairs, much more private and appropriate for a young lady.

WENDY. I don't want to be a young lady.

MRS. DARLING. Which is why you're going to Finishing School.

WENDY. Finishing school?! No I shan't! Why would anyone want a school that *finishes their children*.

  MRS. DARLING. *(Exasperated.)* Wendy.

    WENDY. I've barely started!

MRS. DARLING. Finishing School will prepare you to become the warm wife and doting mother you are destined to be.

WENDY. But what if I'm destined to be like Marie Curie. She's a mother of two and just won a Nobel Prize in Physics!

MRS. DARLING. And does not look very warm in any picture I've seen.

WENDY. Who cares how she looks, she changed the world! And her husband was supposed to get the prize but he insisted *she* get the prize as well, because he believes in her, and I certainly hope that my future "husbandperson" would do the same.

MRS. DARLING. That's lovely.

WENDY. Thank you.

MRS. DARLING. But not likely.

WENDY. *Mother!*

MRS. DARLING. This Curie woman is an exception, my love, and you cannot aspire to that or else everyone would and then no one would be exceptional at all now would they. The only certain thing in life...is growing up.

And going to bed at a reasonable hour.

Michael! John! It's bedtime! You cannot argue with a clock!

>   (**MICHAEL** *with a stuffed crocodile, and* **JOHN** *with a toy sword run on with* **NANA**, *their dog.*)

MICHAEL. No no no. I won't go to bed! I refuse!

JOHN. No bed, no bath, no matter what Nana says.

MRS. DARLING. Nana knows best, boys.

JOHN. Nana eats from a bowl on the floor. I refuse to take orders from a dog!

(**NANA** *barks, the* **BOYS** *immediately straighten up.*)

MICHAEL. Yes Nana.

JOHN. My apologies.

MRS. DARLING. Thank you Nana. Into bed, all of you!

MICHAEL. But Mother, Mother, why must we go to bed *every single day?!*

JOHN. Yes indeed, it's high time we deserved a break.

WENDY. That's what sleeping is, John. It's a break.

MICHAEL. But closing one's eyes for *hours* is terribly exhausting.

WENDY. So is trying to herd all of you into the exact same routine we somehow accomplish every night. Into bed this instant!

MICHAEL.	**JOHN.**
Yes Wendy.	**Yes Wendy.**

(*They go.*)

MRS. DARLING. You see my dear. The way you manage your brothers. You'll be such a good mother one day.

WENDY. Not that anyone bothered to ask if I wanted to.

MRS. DARLING. What was that?

WENDY. Just that…I don't want to think about being a mother, Mother, I want to think about big things like the stars!

MRS. DARLING. (*Trying to mask how much that hurt.*) You don't want to be…like me?

WENDY. Well…I'd just…rather be like *me*.

> (**MR. DARLING** *enters in a fuss, holding an untied shiny white necktie.*)

MR. DARLING. Mary, we *cannot* be late to this party, which I only mention because *we are currently very late to this party.*

MRS. DARLING. I'm coming darling.

MR. DARLING. And this tie simply will not tie! Around the bedpost it will but not around my neck which is rather the ambition of a necktie.

MRS. DARLING. Let me, darling.

> *(She starts to tie his tie.)*

MR. DARLING. We must make a prompt and proud impression or else the retiring chief executive will never promote *me* to chief executive, and what is life but the continual effort to become someone's chief executive!?

> **JOHN.** Hear hear, Father!
>
>> **MR. DARLING.** Thank you very much.

(Just noticing his offspring.) Oh hello, children.

MICHAEL & JOHN.	**WENDY.**
Good evening Papa!	Good evening Father.

MR. DARLING. *(Then instantly scolding.)* Good gracious, what are you still doing awake?! I told you Mary, I told you it was a rough idea to have a dog for a nanny.

> (**NANA** *barks.*)

(To **NANA.***)* Present canines excluded, of course.

MRS. DARLING. Say goodnight to your father children!

JOHN. Father! I've been working on my bravado, like we discussed.

MR. DARLING. Good boy, hurry up, let's see it.

MRS. DARLING. George, you're exciting them.

MR. DARLING. The boy wants to express his bravado, Mary, this is what fathers are for. Go on then, son.

(**JOHN** *strikes a "very manly" pose.*)

JOHN. I do wonder if it's not too intimidating.

WENDY.	**MICHAEL.**
It's not.	I mean…

MR. DARLING. Much improved, John. A bit more with the shoulders, wider legs and I'd experiment with a severe arch in the brow, it's always worked for me. *Let's go, Mary!*

   MRS. DARLING. Yes, darling.

     MICHAEL. Mother, Mother!

       MRS. DARLING. Yes, Michael.

MICHAEL. I have an urgent question. What were my first words?

MRS. DARLING. I think you are trying to stall our departure, but your first words were "mama" and "papa."

WENDY. Everyone's first words are "mama" and "papa."

   MRS. DARLING. Hush dear. He's being adorable.

     MICHAEL. I'm being adorable! What were my next words, Mother?

       MRS. DARLING. Your next was probably "chocolate."

MR. DARLING. And the next was "inheritance" which is why we cannot be late for this party.

MRS. DARLING. Oh George.

(To the children.) Bed, children.

MRS. DARLING. *(To her husband.)* Tie, husband. Don't fiddle with it now that I've fixed it.

MR. DARLING. Oh please, I don't fiddle.

MRS. DARLING.	**WENDY.**
Yes you do.	Yes you do.
You're as bad as John.	

MR. DARLING. *(Striking the identical pose of incredulity.)* I am not as bad as him.

JOHN. He is not as bad as I.

WENDY. Perhaps I do want my own room.

MICHAEL. Your own room?

JOHN. What do you mean, Wendy?

MICHAEL. This *is* your room.

WENDY. Not for long. Mother and Father are moving me out.

JOHN. But where will you go?!

WENDY. Upstairs, apparently.

MICHAEL. *To the roof?!*

MRS. DARLING. No no no. To a private room that is appropriate for a young lady.

JOHN. She's not a young lady, she's a young Wendy.

MICHAEL. But who will tell us stories? I need her stories!

WENDY. I will still tell you stories, and I won't be far away. We'll all simply have to grow up…a bit more on our own.

JOHN. Then it's a very good thing I finalized my defensive posture. Don't worry Father, soon enough I'll be a chief executive and we shall both defend this family on every front.

MR. DARLING. What is it you think I do, my boy?

JOHN. Some form of financial warfare.

MR. DARLING. Dear god, no more upsetting stories for the children, only sobering history.

| **MICHAEL.** | **WENDY.** | **JOHN.** |
| WHAT?! | NO!!! | PAPA!!! |

MRS. DARLING. *(To* **MR. DARLING.***)* You think British history is *less* upsetting? Talk to your daughter.

MR. DARLING. How many words for *late* must I employ?

MRS. DARLING. She's in a rebellion about school. *Now, talk to her, now.*

>   (**NANA** *has smelled* **TINKERBELL** *in the armoire and is scratching at the door.*)

MR. DARLING. Yes yes yes.

(To **WENDY.***)* Wendy dear I'm sure Mother has told you about your new Finishing School for young women.

>   **WENDY.** *(Not excited.)* Yes, Father.

>   **MR. DARLING.** A school that should quite excite you.

>   **WENDY.** *(Not excited.)* Yes, Father.

>   **MR. DARLING.** A school that you should *try and convince me* excites you because it's very expensive.

WENDY. Then perhaps you could transfer the money to a school for the sciences that would actually excite me.

| **MR. DARLING.** | **MRS. DARLING.** | **WENDY.** |
| *(Horrified.)* **Did she say "the sciences?"** | Oh my goodness. | Father, have **you heard of Madame Curie?** |

MRS. DARLING. *Wendy, quiet. Father, exit.* Nana and I must give our goodnights to the children, so we can accelerate the evening.

> (**NANA** *has been harassing and pawing at* **MR. DARLING** *all night and he's fed up.*)

MR. DARLING. *Good gracious!* I think Nana is the source of our late departure and she is spending the night outside.

WENDY.	JOHN.	MICHAEL.
Outside?!	No! Why?	Father no!

MR. DARLING. She's made us late, she's ruining the furniture, and I will not have my boys evermore dependent on a dog for comfort, I'm putting my foot down.

> (*All of the* **CHILDREN** *scream.*)

Not on the *dog*, on the *matter* – good lord.

MRS. DARLING. George is that necessary?

MR. DARLING. We're going to miss the event, the children are screeching. Nana and I are leaving!

> (**MR. DARLING** *takes* **NANA** *from the armoire and starts to exit with her while* **NANA** *barks or wiggles or tries to escape his grasp.*)

WENDY.	JOHN.	MICHAEL.
Father, let her go!	She's only watching over us!	**I can't sleep without Nana!**

MRS. DARLING. George really! *George!*

> (*But he is gone with* **NANA** *who barks and barks.*)

MICHAEL. We didn't even get to say goodnight to Nana. We always say goodnight to Nana!

JOHN. Oh Mother, that is not her happy bark.

(**WENDY** *whips out a notebook and checks it.*)

WENDY. Yes, according to my informal exhaustive survey of Nana's nonverbal communication that is her "intruders are nearby" bark.

MICHAEL. What will we do!?

JOHN. Oh my goodness.

MRS. DARLING. Don't fret, boys. All is quiet and still and safe outside and in.

JOHN. But perhaps we can keep the night lights on tonight? For Michael's sake.

MRS. DARLING. That's a good solution, John. You may relax your posture.

(**JOHN** *stops standing like a crazy person.*)

Everyone to bed this instant, no more dillydallying.

WENDY. Mother, I hope we can further discuss Finishing School. I don't think it is the right place for me –

MRS. DARLING. (*Putting an end to it.*) Wendy. Your job is to grow, my job is to help you. Trust me. And get in bed.

(*All the* **CHILDREN** *jump under their covers.*)

(**WENDY** *takes a magnifying glass to bed, like other girls would take a doll.* **MICHAEL** *takes a great number of teddy bears and one stuffed crocodile to bed.* **JOHN** *takes a toy sword to bed.*)

Goodnight my darling Darlings. Nightlights protect my sleeping children.

> (**MRS. DARLING** *finishes tucking them in, singing this simple lullaby.*)
>
> (*But perhaps she senses a strangeness in the air. She checks the area again, opens the window, closes it but it's not secured.*)

[MUSIC NO. 01 – MOTHER'S LULLABY]

MRS. DARLING. (*Sung.*)
NIGHT LIGHT
BURN BRIGHT
WARM THE ROOM, SLEEPING SOON
NIGHT LIGHT.
STEADFAST
AT LAST.
TIRED EYES, FIRELIGHT
STEADFAST.
PROTECT MY LITTLE ONES, AS THEY DREAM FREE.
BURN BRIGHT, AS THEY GROW UP, ENLIGHTENED BE
MY LOVE
PROUD OF
ALL MY HEART, NEVER PART
MY LOVE.

> (**MRS. DARLING** *exits, closing the door after her.* **WENDY** *utters her own ode.*)

WENDY. (*Determined.*) Nightlights burn bright, and never, never, let us grow up.

> (*The* **CHILDREN** *sleep.*)
>
> (**JOHN** *dreams of being a big brave man.* **MICHAEL** *dreams of animals.* **WENDY** *dreams of…freedom.*)

(Then the window blows open and **PETER PAN** *flies in landing on the window ledge. He looks in and around, then whispers.)*

PETER. Tink? *Tink? Are you here?*

(The armoire rattles. This wakes **WENDY**, *who opens her eyes but doesn't move, overhearing this intrusion but trying to look asleep. She responds to everything they say with incredulity.)*

I said stay away from drawers, didn't I. It's not my fault you're always getting locked in something. Did you find my shadow?

(The armoire rattles and rattles.)

Well hold on. I'm trying, do you think I want you living your life in a cabinet?

(He opens it and the **BALL OF LIGHT** *flies out and around the room. Illuminating lamps, vases, dollhouses, a toy pirate ship and any other thing a* **BALL OF LIGHT** *can fit into.* **TINKERBELL** *flies near* **WENDY** *who gasps or stifles a squeal.)*

*(***PETER** *freezes and flies to the ceiling at the sound of her. She pretends to snore which relaxes him. He flies over the* **CHILDREN** *and investigates them.)*

Very curious.

(Hovering over **JOHN**.*)* This one is dreaming of swordfights even though he's made very nervous by swords...and fights.

(Hovering over **MICHAEL**.*)* This one is dreaming of crocodiles and other creatures with unfriendly smiles.

PETER. *(Hovering over* **WENDY**.*)* And this one is...odd. I can't tell what she's dreaming. Stars and flying lights and...things that glow.

> *(***TINKERBELL*** squeaks alerting him to the drawer where his shadow is kept.)*

You found it?! Locked in the drawer? What a terrible thing to do to a shadow. A drawer is nothing but shadows, it must be so crowded.

> *(***TINKERBELL*** tinkles like a little bell in agreement.)*

On my mark. One....two...three open catch him! Shadow! Come here! *Shadow!*

> *(He opens the drawer and out zooms his very own* **SHADOW***! The* **SHADOW** *is wild about the room. It becomes all different shapes until* **PETER** *grabs it by the foot and it returns to* **PETER***'s form. It wiggles and flails as* **PETER** *tries to jam, tie or stick his* **SHADOW** *onto his foot.)*

Shadow! Yes I'm talking to you. We're supposed to stick together, you and I and you are very much *not sticking*.

(To **TINKERBELL**.*)* Help me, Tink.

> *(***TINKERBELL*** tries to help but* **PETER** *accidentally elbows her back in the armoire, which shuts and locks her in again.)*

(To **SHADOW**.*)* I said *stick*, you're a shadow, and you're mine, and you can be no one else's shadow but mine and – and –

(Less angry and more sad.) You *have* to stay with me. You're the only thing I still have that I was born with. And if I don't have you, I'll be...alone. And I won't be made to be anything I don't want to be... SO *STICK*!

(That was a bit more honest than he'd intended.)

*(**WENDY** sits up at this. **PETER** startles.)*

WENDY. Alright this is just ridiculous. You come in our room in the middle of the night, you crash all about, and what do you even mean your shadow isn't sticking?! That's absurd, it's –

*(Seeing the unstuck **SHADOW**.)*

What is that?

(She is shocked.)

PETER. It's my shadow. Hello.

WENDY. Hello. That's your shadow.

PETER. Yes.

WENDY. It's not in the right place.

PETER. That's the problem.

*(**WENDY** takes out her magnifying glass and investigates the **SHADOW**.)*

WENDY. How fabulously strange.

PETER. Thank you.

WENDY. You're welcome, which begs the question: Who *are* you?

PETER. Peter Pan is my name. Who are you?

WENDY. Wendy Moira Angela Darling.

PETER. That's probably too many names. Where do you come from?

WENDY. Here. Where do you come from?

PETER. There. Can you help me with my shadow?

WENDY. I don't know, I've never had much trouble with them myself.

PETER. *Well there's no need to brag about it.*

(He pouts.)

WENDY. *Alright, alright, calm down,* there must be a way to get it stitched on again. I'll help you if you can mange to be *quiet*. My brothers are just there.

PETER. *(Not quiet at all.)* Stitched! Yes, would you sew it on for me?

WENDY. *I said quiet!* And you can't sew a shadow. A shadow is light and dark, and a needle is metal and –

(An idea.)

Wait, I have a thought. Perhaps we could use the *shadow* of the needle to sew the *shadow* of the – you! Doesn't make perfect sense but it's worth a try.

PETER. Oh I think a try is worth everything.

WENDY. Very well.

*(**WENDY** runs to find a needle and thread.)*

Sit still.

*(**WENDY** takes **PETER**'s foot but **PETER** flinches –)*

PETER. Oh no, you must never touch me.

WENDY. I'm sorry. Why can no one touch you?

PETER. Because no one touches me! Well, one person did and I cut off his hand for it.

WENDY. *You cut off a person's hand?! What sort of madman are you?!*

PETER. Don't worry, he was a pirate Captain, it was midbattle, these things happen.

WENDY. Alright, Cheeky. Foot. Up. Now.

> (**PETER** *raises his foot as* **WENDY** *puts the needle and thread in front of the lamp creating its shadow on the wall. She uses the needle's shadow to "sew"* **PETER***'s shadow back to* **PETER***'s foot.)*

PETER. Are you the one that tells the stories?

WENDY. Yes, one or two each night to my brothers.

PETER. Wow. I love stories. They're the beginning and end of everything. We don't have them where I live so I have to come all the way here to bring them back.

WENDY. Where do you live that doesn't have stories?

PETER. Second star to the right and straight on till morning. That's how you get to Neverland.

WENDY. Neverland? What sort of place is that?

PETER. Any sort we want it to be.

WENDY. Who's we?

PETER. The Lost Boys and I! I bring stories to Neverland and it fills up with the most amazing things for us. Whenever I hear an exciting story I think – "Oooh that's a good idea, we should have that in Neverland." And then we do! Magical creatures? Of course. Adventure? Every day. Irresponsible behavior with no consequence? Obviously. It's perfect.

WENDY. It does sound...compelling. But why are the *Lost* Boys lost?

PETER. Because they ran away from their parents like I did so I brought them to Neverland where we can do whatever we like.

WENDY. Whatever you like?!

PETER. Oh yes, the instant my mother held me up as a baby and said "He'll grow up to be a chief executive like his father!" and I said "No I won't, I'll never grow up!" And when she told me a bedtime story about fairies and pirates that night in my cradle and I thought "that's more like it! Take me to the fairies!" And then a fairy said "Okay!" and off we went to Neverland.

WENDY. I have so many questions.

PETER. Honestly I don't know what a chief executive is either.

(She's done sewing his shadow.)

WENDY. Alright you. Up we go, Peter Pan. Let's test our hypothesis and see if your shadow is re-stuck.

*(**PETER** stands and makes movements that his shadow mirrors! It worked!)*

PETER. Whoa! It worked! Look at this! My shadow is back! I did it!

WENDY. *You* did what exactly?

PETER. Everyone knows a boy's shadow obeys the boy.

WENDY. Well "the boy" should realize that he shouldn't take credit for someone else's work. OUT. NOW.

PETER. NoNoNo I'm sorry I'm sorry, Wendy Moira Whatever-The-Other-One-Was Darling, I'm from a land of all boys and I forgot what I vaguely recall as manners and everyone knows that a girl is worth twenty boys.

Some days twenty-five.

WENDY. Uh huh.

    PETER. That was brilliant what you did.

        WENDY. Uh huh.

            PETER. And I thank you. Very much.

(**WENDY** *studies him, then accepts this.*)

WENDY. You're welcome. And you…you've been here before haven't you? In this room?

PETER. Oh well outside of it, many times. I like your stories. We don't have those in Neverland – I said that – and you tell your brothers all the good ones, like the one about the lady scientist with the glowing metal and her – (*He pronounces "Nobel" wrong.*) – noble prize. That one's my favorite.

WENDY. Mine too. And it's Nobel.

PETER. Is it?

WENDY. Yes, and that story isn't a fairytale, it's real. That's why I like it, because it's not about magic, it's about truth.

PETER. Magic is true in Neverland.

(**WENDY** *scoffs at this.*)

You don't believe me?

WENDY. I'm a scientist. I don't have to believe anything I can't prove.

PETER. Aren't I proof enough?

WENDY. (*A great idea is dawning in her.*) Perhaps you could be! Which is why you're going to make a terribly impressive report for the Royal Society, and then my parents will simply *have* to allow me to go to a school for the sciences instead of some finishing school and then…I'll be free!

Can I give you a piece of advice, Peter Pan?

PETER. (*Taking her magnifying glass.*) Ohh sure, is it heavy?

WENDY. No that's not – It's this: stay in Neverland. Stay free. This world does everything it can to hold us down.

PETER. That's why I learned to fly.

Now what does this advice of yours do again?

WENDY. It helps you see what's really there.

> (**PETER** *looks at* **WENDY** *through the glass.* **WENDY** *looks at him the other way.*)

PETER. I see...an explorer. What do you see?

WENDY. A mischief maker.

PETER. Wow this thing really works. Now let me give *you* something.

> (*He reaches in his pockets until he finds...a glowing stone that shines brightly.*)

It's the oldest stone in Neverland. It knows a lot, but only tells a little. You have to listen very closely to hear what it has to say...

> (**WENDY** *gasps when she sees it. She snatches back her magnifying glass to inspect it.*)

WENDY. It's beautiful!

PETER. *(Re: the magnifying glass.)* And you've taken your own advice.

> (**WENDY** *marvels at it, puts it to her ear, listens...*)

WENDY. SHHH. It says that...that you *are* the boy that never grows up. And that Neverland *is* real.

PETER. I mean the rock knows. Trust the rock.

> *(Goes for it.)*

And come with me. To Neverland. Tonight.

WENDY. Tonight? But I –

*(Then **TINKERBELL** rattles the drawer she's locked in. **WENDY** startles. **PETER** wields the magnifying glass like a sword. Then remembers.)*

PETER. Oh! My fairy! Forgot about her. She's gone and locked herself in a drawer again.

*(He flings open the drawer and out flies **TINKERBELL** sputtering a string of bell sounds.)*

WENDY. That's the thing I was just chasing around the room.

PETER. That would explain all the names she's calling you.

*(To **WENDY**.)* She gets upset when there are other girls around and she doesn't like that you're coming back with us.

*(**TINKERBELL** freaks out at this idea.)*

WENDY. I'm not going with you, I can't.

PETER. But you must! You know stories, we need stories. You want freedom, we've got freedom.

*(To **TINKERBELL**.) Hush, Tink.*

*(To **WENDY**.)* You want to prove something to the world? Do it. You're brilliant, you're brave, the stone likes you. Come on. Don't be held down. Fly with me!

WENDY. I don't know if I should –

*(**TINKERBELL** freaks out more.)*

PETER. Yes you do. You don't want to stay here and be – what was it – finished?

*(This hits **WENDY**. She is not done.)*

WENDY. I would…very much like to go I think. Yes. Yes I would. Let's go. I think.

PETER. I think you think right.

> (**TINKERBELL** *is pissed.*)

(Tink this is happening I need you to get behind this.)

WENDY. But I need to take my brothers with me. I can't leave them.

PETER. Bring them! The more the crazier! I can teach all of you to fly, all you need is fairy dust and the very end of your last dream which is.

> (*Mentally reading them in this order:* **JOHN**, **MICHAEL**, **WENDY**.)

Battle, croc, and something called Radium.

> (**WENDY** *wakes her brothers.*)

WENDY. Let's do it. John! Michael! Wake up.

PETER. Wake up, boys. Adventure, calling.

JOHN. What's going on? What's all this?

MICHAEL. But Wendy, I'm *tiiiiiired*.

WENDY. Not for long, there's a boy here and he can fly and he's going to teach us to fly and we're all going to Neverland to have scientifically fulfilling adventures this instant.

MICHAEL. *(So sleepy.)* That makes very little sense.

JOHN. *WHO IS THAT?*

PETER. Hello boys, I'm Peter Pan.

JOHN. *WHAT IS THAT?*

PETER. I'll be your captain for today's flight.

MICHAEL. Is this really happening?

WENDY. Yes! Get up! Go find your shoes, boys. Hurry!

(The following bold section is needed only if your production requires actors to get into flying harnesses. If you are not using harnesses you may omit and pick up after this section.)

*(**WENDY** runs off to get her notebook and bag – and to get in her flying harness.)*

*(**MICHAEL** runs off to find his shoes – and get into his flying harness. **NANA** barks and barks outside.)*

JOHN. Oh nonono, Nana doesn't like this and neither do I.

PETER. But you will once we get there! Adventure, fun –

WENDY. Shoes, John!

PETER. Yes we have some of those too.

*(**JOHN** goes behind the curtains or the bed to find his shoes – and also get into his flying harnesses.)*

MICHAEL. I can only find *one* shoe, Wendy!

WENDY. Check the closet!

MICHAEL. I'm *in* the closet. Oh wait, *found them!*

JOHN. What will Mother and Father think? I don't like this subterfuge. Or heights. Or strangers!

PETER. Come on John. Neverland has something for everyone.

MICHAEL. Even scaredy cats.

JOHN. *I'm not scared, I'm understandably cautious.*

(**WENDY** *returns and grabs her notebook and pencil for the journey.*)

WENDY. Alright! I've got my magnifying glass, notebook, pencil and two brothers. Let's go!

MICHAEL.　　　　　　　**JOHN.**
YAY!　　　　　　　　　　Oh my goodness.

PETER. Well then we just need to sprinkle a bit of fairy dust...

(**PETER** *grabs* **TINKERBELL** *and shakes her over the* **CHILDREN** *sprinkling golden dust on them.*)

And think a few of your happiest thoughts and...

(**PETER** *starts to rise in front of them.*)

JOHN.　　　　　　　　**MICHAEL.**
Good heavens, he's flying.　Whoaaaaa...

WENDY. I told you!

PETER. But the most important part is to say out loud with all your bravery, you say... "I'm free."

(*And with that* **PETER** *really flies around the room! He's amazing!*)

(*The* **CHILDREN** *are amazed and excited!*)

WENDY. That's it? Just say...I'm free!

(*And* **WENDY** *rises and starts flying. She's cautious but committed.*)

PETER. That's it! Brava!

MICHAEL. *Me too! Me too! I'm free too! I'm so freeeee!*

(*And* **MICHAEL** *rises and flies about the room, bumping into walls and giggling.*)

JOHN. Wendy wait! Shouldn't we ask Mother and Father about the flying?

WENDY. They wouldn't understand. Come on John!

MICHAEL. John, come on!

JOHN. *(Totally nervous.)* Well I – I wouldn't want to leave you unguarded. So – I suppose – I'm free – sort of?

> *(And **JOHN** jerks up and flies wildly about the room.)*

PETER.	MICHAEL.	WENDY.
Well done, John!	John's flying too!	Wonderful!

> *(They fly as much as you like. **NANA** starts barking down the hall.)*

MICHAEL.	JOHN.	WENDY.
Look at me!	***This is unexpectedly amusing!***	Isn't this lovely!

PETER. Now all you have to do is leap into the night air, jump on the wind, and follow the friendliest stars to Neverland. Stay close to me, don't look back and away we go.

> *(And the whole crew jumps off the window ledge and into the night.)*

Transition

The Stars

(The **CHILDREN**, **PETER**, *and* **TINKERBELL** *fly through the night. It's exhilarating. It's beautiful.)*

WENDY. Isn't this tremendous! It's simply –

MICHAEL. Amazing!

JOHN. Terrifying!

WENDY. – not aerodynamically sound but somehow here we are!

PETER. "Somehow" is my entire philosophy. Come on!

WENDY. And the stars! Look at them! The parallax shift from this height is fascinating. Could we stop so I can make a few notes?

PETER. We can't stop, we're almost there now! Everyone, keep going, don't get lost and don't listen to the comets. They have no idea what they're talking about.

Onwards!

*(***PETER** *crows as he,* **JOHN**, *and* **MICHAEL** *hurry on as* **WENDY** *tries to make notes her in notebook. They speed off without her making a big turn. When* **WENDY** *looks up she sees...she's alone.)*

WENDY. Peter? Wait, where did they go ? *Peter! Peter!*

(She sees **TINKERBELL** *fly by.)*

Tinkerbell, wait! I don't know which way they've flown. Which way do I go?

> *(But **TINKERBELL** flies in all sorts of ways spinning **WENDY** all around, disorienting her.)*

I don't know what you're saying. Please just show me – point, blink, for heaven's sake *pinch* the way to Neverland.

> *(But **TINKERBELL** makes a little obnoxious tinkle sound and speeds off without her.)*

TINK! You can't leave me like this, I'm all turned around, I don't know where to go! *Please!*

> *(But **WENDY** is alone. She consults her notebook...)*

Alright stars. Start talking.

> *(...and flies off on her own.)*

ACT TWO

Scene One

Neverland, Pirate Ship

*(Before we see the wonderful lush expanse of Neverland, we meet our nemesis, **CAPTAIN HOOK**, and his sidekick **SMEE**, sitting in the cramped, dark, wooden office of Hook's pirate ship.)*

*(The walls are covered with crocodile heads, taxidermied as trophies. **CAPTAIN HOOK** has been killing any croc he sees trying to find the one that hunts him.)*

*(**CAPTAIN HOOK** paces like a panther, ready to pounce at any moment. He's furious, steaming. **SMEE** is a nervous "yes" man, constantly tidying, checking things off a list, polishing the crocs and trying not to be killed today.)*

SMEE. As you can see, Captain, night watch caught two crocs, but found no clock in either. The clock being the signifier of the specific beast that ate your hand, liked it so much, it wants the rest, which if you really think about it, is a compliment, sir.

*(**CAPTAIN HOOK** slams his handless arm on the table making **SMEE** flinch.)*

CAPTAIN HOOK. It is a curse not a compliment. That sound, Smee. Tick tock, tick tock. It haunts me: dreaming, waking, all because Pan got one good strike.

SMEE. He did get the upper hand. Though I think a battle scar makes you far more intimidating, if I may say.

CAPTAIN HOOK. You may not. The thought never leaves me that in mere moments that monster ripped through my ship, my room, ravenous, insatiable, fanged jaws ready to swallow me whole –

SMEE. – but instead swallowing the clock by your bed, due to me chucking it at its horrifying face. My finest hour, sir. Clocked that croc for you once and I'd do it again.

CAPTAIN HOOK. I don't want it clocked, I want it gutted, skinned, and mounted on my *wall*.

SMEE. Of course sir. We'll keep our eyes peeled.

CAPTAIN HOOK. Do that or else I will have to peel your eyes myself.

SMEE. That is a vivid image sir.

CAPTAIN HOOK. *And yet the image I long to see is Pan, caught and caged in the belly of this ship.* WHERE IS HE?!

SMEE. Trying sir! Every day sir! We did net two score of those lighty up fairies just like his Tinkerbell, but when they wouldn't talk we bottled 'em up for target practice. Little ladies explode like fireworks if you hit 'em straight on, *"fairyworks"* if you like.

CAPTAIN HOOK. I don't.

SMEE. To each their own, sir. In further news some of the crew had a tussle over an orange, but I made sure the fruit survived only slightly bruised. Also a few of them mermaids tried to sneak in the portholes.

CAPTAIN HOOK. Kill them.

SMEE. Yessir. Pests really, mermaids.

CAPTAIN HOOK. Kill the *crew*.

SMEE. The crew sir? Again sir?

CAPTAIN HOOK. If they find time to tussle over an orange this makes them thieves of my time, which makes them thieves of my *life*, thus they will pay *with theirs*.

SMEE. That is a deeply rational response, sir. Time is the only thing that matters. You cannot argue with a clock.

CAPTAIN HOOK. *The only thing that matters is the boy.* We cannot control this place if we do not control him; What of The Lost Boys and do not tell me that they are lost.

SMEE. It does seem self-evident, but we can't find them.

CAPTAIN HOOK. I am drowning in a sea of incompetence.

SMEE. Good news of the native clans though: our raids seem to have run them off for good, save the girl Tiger Lily, but she's no trouble, being as I mentioned, a girl.

CAPTAIN HOOK. The girl is useless, Pan is the key to Neverland. I *need* that boy.

SMEE. It is an odd feeling to so much need the thing you so much hate.

>   (**CAPTAIN HOOK** *slams/breaks/rages at something. That pissed him off.*)

CAPTAIN HOOK. Smee.

SMEE. Yessir.

CAPTAIN HOOK. Let us never say that again.

SMEE. Yessir.

CAPTAIN HOOK. My hook.

SMEE. Yessir.

*(**SMEE** retrieves and presents the Captain's hook. **CAPTAIN HOOK** takes it and slowly, steadily, squeakily twists it into its base on his handless forearm.)*

SMEE. About the crew, Captain –

CAPTAIN HOOK. YesYes, you needn't kill them after all.

SMEE. Thank you sir, it always makes such a mess.

CAPTAIN HOOK. I'll do it myself this time.

SMEE. I'll get the mop.

*(**CAPTAIN HOOK** grabs a menacing sword and heads off for a bit of gleeful murder as **SMEE** tags along after and the lights transition us to...)*

[MUSIC NO. 02 – PIRATE SONG]

PIRATES.
WE SAIL, WE FIGHT WITH ALL OUR MIGHT,
AND IF WE DIE, THE TIME WAS RIGHT,
WE'LL MEET AGAIN BELOW.
WE'LL MEET AGAIN BELOW.
OUR FLAGS ARE RED, SO WATCH YOUR HEAD
'CAUSE IF WE FIND YA, YOU'LL BE DEAD,
AND UNDERSEA YOU'LL GO.
AND UNDERSEA YOU'LL GO.

Scene Two

Neverland Forest

(And now we open up to the fullness of wild, wonderful Neverland. This is the place of dreams and fantasy, bedtime stories and myths. It's a riveting, fun place. Until it's not. This place can turn on you, like any dream. It's always dusk or dawn here. The light is always abundant with color. The plants are always moving. The trees are many and both beautiful and dark. The sky shimmers.)

(There are corners to this place, hidden doors, secrets.)

(Out of one of these hidden doors or swinging in on a rope or some other magnificent entrance – comes **TIGER LILY**. *She is a real kickass kinda girl. Strong, self-sufficient, vigilant. She knows how to take care of herself because she has to. Her clothing has some magic to it – it can change to what camouflages her best. Wood, starlight, water. This is* her *land and it's been taken over by* **CAPTAIN HOOK**, *and she wants it respected and wants it back.)*

(She scans the sky and the land. She whistles at something.)

*(***JEROME THE CROCODILE*** emerges, lumbers through the trees. It's rather massive. It makes a tick tock sounds because, as you know, it swallowed a clock. It also growls and roars in feelings.)*

TIGER LILY. *(Petting and scratching him like a good sweet dog.)* Who's a good boy, who is it, you're a good boy. That's right, it's you, It's my big buddy!

> (**TIGER LILY** *looks up at the stars. Notices something.*)

Shhh. Pirates...

> (**TIGER LILY** *whistles to the* **CROCODILE** *who stops. They both hear something in the distance.*)

[MUSIC NO. 2A – PIRATE SONG]

PIRATES.
THE OCEAN GROANS INSIDE OUR BONES
AND HOLLERS OUT FOR DAVY JONES,
WHO WAITS FOR US BELOW.
WHO WAITS FOR US BELOW.

TIGER LILY. God I'd wish they would get a new song.

> *(The* **CROCODILE** *growls in agreement.)*

Right? I mean they think they're so tough and they just sing off-key all day.

I don't know how *you* follow them around all the time but I couldn't do it –

> *(The* **CROCODILE** *growls.)*

I get that but come on, you ate *one* hand, how could you even get a real taste for it. You're mouth is big enough to fit *minimum* two goats.

> *(The* **CROCODILE** *growls.)*

Okay, it was the best hand you ever had. I'm just saying I think we're coming at this whole "defeat Captain Hook" thing from two very different sides. I'm here to avenge my people and you just want a snack.

*(The **CROCDILE** growls in protest.)*

I know, I know, you've got my back, I've got yours. It's you and me, kiddo.

*(The **CROCODILE** appreciates this. They are friends.)*

Either way we've gotta get that clock out of you, buddy. It's a real giveaway.

Wait. Something's coming!

*(**TIGER LILY** shushes the **CROCODILE**, who gulps and the clock's noise dims a bit. **TIGER LILY** and the **CROCODILE** hide somewhere and wait.)*

*(Of course who comes onto the path first? The **LOST BOYS**. They climb out of their underground house and look to the sky. **TIGER LILY** watches them, peeved that they're definitely going to ruin her plan. The **LOST BOYS** are: **SLIGHTLY**, **TOOTLES**, **CURLY**.)*

SLIGHTLY. Did you hear Peter? Is he back?

TOOTLES. I thought I heard him crow! Love when he does that.

> **SLIGHTLY**. Iconic.
>
> > **CURLY**. I told you he'd come back.
> >
> > > **TOOTLES**. I do hope he brought us more stories. We're almost out!

SLIGHTLY. The woman at the orphanage used to tell us stories.

CURLY. Really! Which ones?!

SLIGHTLY. Mostly the one that goes:

SLIGHTLY. *(Quoting his exhausted orphanage minder.)* "Put that down, young man. Not on your sister, on the floor! And wherever are your pants? Goodness gracious they're slightly soiled! Heaven help me, I'm losing my sense with all these children!"

CURLY.	**TOOTLES**.
That's a beautiful story.	Wooooooooow.

SLIGHTLY. That's how I got the name Slightly...Soiled, at least I think that's my name, she said that a lot around me.

TOOTLES. I have no idea why they call me Tootles.

SLIGHTLY.	**CURLY**.
We do.	It's cause you smell bad.

*(**TIGER LILY** leaps into the middle of the **BOYS**. They scream. She silences them.)*

TIGER LILY. *HEY. Dingbats.* Crocodile that way, pirates that way. Go back underground.

TOOTLES. Oh no we won't, we're waiting for Peter.

CURLY. He'll want us at the ready when he comes back.

TIGER LILY. But he's not here and the pirates will be. GO.

    SLIGHTLY. No.

        TIGER LILY. *Now.*

            TOOTLES. *No. We wait for Peter.*

                TIGER LILY. You do recall that my first name is *Tiger.*

                    CURLY. I do, it's very intimidating.

                        TIGER LILY. Under. Ground. *Now.*

(But before they can, the "Pirate Song" is suddenly loud and close!)

[MUSIC NO. 02B – PIRATE SONG]

CURLY. **SLIGHTLY.** **TOOTLES.**
Where is Peter? Go go go! Pirates! Run!
We need Peter!

(The BOYS scatter, dropping a wooden sword, a doll made of sticks, and a folded piece of paper. TIGER LILY and the CROCODILE hurry to hide.)

PIRATES.
WE CROSS THE SEAS, TAKE WHAT WE PLEASE
AND IF YOU CROSS US, ON YOUR KNEES!
WE'LL SEND YOU DOWN BELOW.
WE'LL SEND YOU DOWN BELOW.

(Just as the PIRATE CREW walk on swords drawn, just chatting it up.)

JUKES. You know my mum got my sword customized right before I left.

NOODLER. Did she really?

JUKES. Yeah she had 'em etch a little message in the blade: "Slay all day, love mum"

NOODLER. Awwwwwww.

STARKEY. That is so thoughtful.

JUKES. I think of her every time I go in for the kill. And because she was a vicious woman.

NOODLER. Oh! Found something sir!

(SMEE spots the folded paper slightly left and picks it up.)

SMEE. What is it, what's this?

NOODLER. It's a note.

STARKEY. It's a note!

JUKES. And there's a map on it!

NOODLER. No, it's a symbol of some kind.

STARKEY. It's a...?

JUKES. Is that a...?

NOODLER. Is that a rump?

SMEE. It's a heart, you idiots. Flip it round.

(They turn it upside down.)

STARKEY.	**NOODLER.**	**JUKES.**
Ohhhh **It's a heart**.	I see it now	Yeah It's a heart. Got it.

SMEE. "You are never alone, son. Love Mum."

STARKEY. Isn't that nice.

NOODLER. That's good parenting.

JUKES. But wait sir. We ain't got mums in Neverland.

SMEE. It's not the note *belonging to* a mum, it's a note *originating with a* mum.

STARKEY. Oh oh! If this is the note of a *boy* there might be more of them nearby, and more than one boy is called *boys,* and since they're missing as well these might / be the Lost –

SMEE. *The Lost Boys, they're the Lost Boys, we're way ahead of you,* and if we can find their lair, we find Pan. And Captain wants him *dead*.

    JUKES. Dead's good.

        STARKEY. I can work with dead.

            NOODLER. I love dead.

                SMEE. *WAIT.*

(**SMEE** *and the others hear an ominous Tick Tock from the approaching* **CROCODILE**. *It chills him to the bone. He freezes.*)

Oh no. No no no.

STARKEY. Sir.

SMEE. Shh.

STARKEY. I hear something.

SMEE. *I know that's why I said: SHH!*

JUKES. It's the tick.

NOODLER. It's the tock.

STARKEY. It's the croc that swallowed the clock!

SMEE. Which I told you to *kill* yesterday!

JUKES. Oh right so –

NOODLER. We did not do that.

STARKEY. Way too big.

JUKES. Way too fast.

NOODLER. Way too many teeth.

SMEE. *I am drowning in a sea of incompetence.* I really wish Captain hadn't made me kill the last crew.

(*This crew looks nervous at that last remark.*)

NOODLER. I thought they went on holiday.

SMEE. *They didn't.*

(*The bushes or reeds shake on two sides of the* **PIRATES**. *They scream.*)

JUKES. I thought the croc was after the Captain, not us!

SMEE. I don't know if it has a perfectly discerning pirate palate!

STARKEY. I still don't understand why an amphibious predator such as himself would eat a clock?

JUKES. Valid question.

NOODLER. It's an odd choice for a carnivore.

*(The swoosh from the **CROCODILE**'s massive tail swipes the reeds – scream – and the **PIRATES** run for their lives.)*

SMEE.	**JUKES.**	**NOODLER.**	**STARKEY.**
Oh god it's right behind me!	KEEP RUNNING.	AHHHHH	Go, go go go!

*(Once the **PIRATES** are gone, **TIGER LILY** and the **LOST BOYS**, giggling, emerge.)*

TIGER LILY. Oh man, I love when they run.

I mean why even come to Neverland if you can't handle giant semi-aquatic reptiles, am I right?

*(The **CROCODILE** growls in agreement.)*

Go get 'em buddy.

*(And with a swish of its massive tail it exits after the **PIRATES**.)*

TOOTLES. Are you really friends with that crocodile?

TIGER LILY. I mean not at first, but you can be friends with anything that wants what you want. And then when I got to know him, he's actually a big softie, kinda self conscious, you know. I keep telling him, "You're beautiful, you're strong, you can eat anything you want!"

SLIGHTLY. And you can understand what he's saying?

TIGER LILY. I know, "Native girl speaks with animals" but what are you gonna do? Jerome's a sweetheart, super funny, misunderstood really. Hard to get beyond the teeth and make friends.

CURLY. I get that. Nobody wanted to be my friend until Peter.

SLIGHTLY. Me neither!

TOOTLES. Me neither! Peter is our best and first and only friend!

TIGER LILY. Okay, that's super sad you guys. You need to branch out. For croc's sake, I'll be your friend.

TOOTLES. But aren't you – how to put this – no fun?

TIGER LILY. What?

SLIGHTLY. You see we're very committed to fun and you're very committed to serious.

TIGER LILY. Oh come on, you can fight injustice and still be fun. I do lots of fun things.

CURLY. Are the fun things you do mostly with crocodiles?

TIGER LILY. Okay but crocodiles are really fun.

CURLY.	**SLIGHTLY**.	**TOOTLES**.
See, your fun is scary.	I'm gonna go with a no.	Oh I like her.

(We hear **PETER***'s crow! The* **LOST BOYS** *look to the sky!)*

SLIGHTLY. That's Peter!! Look!

   CURLY. Peter's back!

      TOOTLES. It's Peter and Tink and some lumpy sort of birds!

SLIGHTLY. Thank goodness he's back, I was getting so worried.

TIGER LILY. He was gone for *one* night, guys. Calm down.

CURLY. Watch out!

> (**TINKERBELL'S BALL OF LIGHT** *soars down like a comet and lands somewhere behind the bushes, kicking up sparks.*)

PETER. Come in for a landing!

JOHN.	**MICHAEL.**
You didn't tell us how to land!	We're here! We're here!

> (**PETER, JOHN** *and* **MICHAEL** *all land too. The boys marvel at the place.*)

TOOTLES.	**CURLY.**	**SLIGHTLY.**
Peter! Yes!	You're back!	**We were not worried at all.**

PETER. Hey there, Boys. Let's welcome some new friends to Neverland.

CURLY.	**SLIGHTLY.**	**TOOTLES.**
Welcome to Neverland!	It's so great.	**You're gonna love it.**

MICHAEL. Oh my word, it's amazing!

JOHN. *(Very nervous.)* I am amazed.

PETER. It's the best of places with everything you've ever dreamed of:

  CURLY. mermaids

    SLIGHTLY. and fairies

      TOOTLES. and jungles and oceans!

TIGER LILY. Except that Hook is destroying everything you just mentioned and you leave to fly around every night.

PETER PAN. And then there's Tiger Lily. She's like a cousin that you have to hang out with.

TIGER LILY. I'm like your babysitter but I don't get paid.

JOHN. Is she a princess?

TIGER LILY. My people don't have princesses. We have real girls with real skills.

PETER. Defeat any pirates today?

   TIGER LILY. About two minutes ago.

      PETER. How's Jerome?

         TIGER LILY. Living and loving.

           PETER. Ready to save Neverland?

              TIGER LILY. Always.

                 PETER. Nice.

(They smile and do an elaborate handshake but never actually touch hands. They're actually friends.)

MICHAEL. Excuse me, Mr. Pan, have you seen our sister?

PETER. What? Wendy's not here?

JOHN. She was flying right beside me.

MICHAEL. And behind me.

JOHN. But now she's nowhere and she's lost and what do we do?!

*(**TINKERBELL** emerges from the bushes, human-sized, no longer a ball of light but still magically glowing top to toe.)*

LOST BOYS.	**TINKERBELL.**
TINKERBELL!!!!!	Heyyyyyyy, boys!!!!

(She walks in demanding applause in that fake "no don't applaud but really you have to applaud" way. The **LOST BOYS** *applaud...* **TIGER** *doesn't.)*

TINKERBELL. OhMyGodYou'reSoSweetNoReallyDon't ButDo! OK! Party starting, what are we doing? I could eat.

PETER. Tink...

TINKERBELL. MmmHmm.

PETER. ...erbell.

TINKERBELL. MmmHmm.

PETER. Where's Wendy?

TINKERBELL. I don't know, why would I know, she got lost in the stars, it's a big place.

PETER. TINK.

TINKERBELL. I didn't do anything! I would never hurt a friend of Peter's, or send her spiraling into the vastness of space.

TIGER LILY. You might want to do something about your fairy? She's getting a little murdery.

TINKERBELL. *Hey.*

PETER. *TINK, Wendy was our friend.*

TINKERBELL. Which is why I'm super bummed that she's floating in an airless void, but I mean look, that Wendy thing was obviously not tough enough for Neverland okay. She's lacking that je ne sais quoi – which is French – plus we have way too many girls here already.

TIGER LILY. There's literally just me.

TINKERBELL. *Waaaaaaaay* too many girls. WendyThing was never going to make it here, Peter.

*(Of course **WENDY** enters stomping through the jungle, twigs in her hair, dirt on her face, gown ripped.)*

WENDY. And yet HERE I AM. HELLO, NEVERLAND.

PETER, MICHAEL & JOHN. **LOST BOYS.**
Wendy!   *Whoaaaaaaaaa!*

MICHAEL. You made it!

JOHN. Thank goodness you're alright!

TINKERBELL. *(Super bummed.)* OhMyGodShe'sHere yaaaaayyyyyy.

MICHAEL. We were so worried.

PETER. What happened?

WENDY. *That fairy happened.* She pushed me off course and left me for dead.

TINKERBELL. That was a very different fairy.

WENDY. I know a grown up ball of traitorous light when I see one. She lies, she pinches, she tried to kill me!

TIGER LILY. That is very on brand for her.

TINKERBELL. HEY.

PETER. We've talked about this Tink!

TINKERBELL. I'm defending you, Peter.

PETER. Well stop!

TINKERBELL. EXCUSE ME?

PETER. Tink, just give us some space please.

TINKERBELL. I just gave her all the space in outer space and now you want more space?! Oh you have messed with the wrong fairy, there is no greater power than a lady with wings and a vendetta. WAY TOO MANY GIRLS.

(*Angrily,* **TINKERBELL** *storms – or flies – off.*)

TIGER LILY. Hi there, Tiger Lily, so far I think you're pretty cool.

WENDY. Thank you, Wendy, is this place always so perilous?

TIGER LILY. I mean my best friend is a crocodile so pretty much yeah.

JOHN. Oh I am not prepared for this.

MICHAEL. I am! What fun!

PETER. I'm so sorry about Tink, Wendy. How did you find us?

WENDY. I rocked on.

(*She pulls out the stone* **PETER** *gave her.*)

The stone told me the way.

(*To the stone.*) And thank you very much, you are a scholar and a gentleman.

TOOTLES. Is she the new mother, Peter?!

    PETER. Oh well, um –

        WENDY. The what?

            TIGER LILY. A mother? She's a kid.

CURLY.	**SLIGHTLY.**	**TOOTLES.**
You're the new mother?	She's perfect!	**Do you have any snacks?**

WENDY. *A mother?* No no no, I'm *not* a mother. Peter, tell them. I'm just a girl who likes astronomy.

TOOTLES. But you promised us a mother.

CURLY. You promised, Peter!

SLIGHTLY. Someone to clean, and cook, and fix our socks and make pudding and remember how each of us likes our tea?!

WENDY. You did what?

PETER. I didn't *promise them*. I said I'd investigate the possibility.

WENDY. And I can confirm that possibility is zero. *I'm here for an adventure of my own not to wipe your noses!*

(The **BOYS** *are shocked. One of them sneezes.)*

CURLY. *(Innocently chauvinistic.)* But isn't that what girls are supposed to do?

WENDY & TIGER LILY. *No it's not what girls are supposed to do.*

WENDY. They're supposed to be strong –

> **TIGER LILY.** And brilliant –
>> **WENDY.** And explore the world –
>>> **TIGER LILY.** And defend it –
>>>> **WENDY.** And find the truth of things –
>>>>> **TIGER LILY.** And spend lots of quality time with crocodiles.

WENDY. What? Sure. You rascals don't need a mother, you need some common sense.

CURLY. And where does that grow?

TIGER LILY. Not on this island.

(To **WENDY.***)* Quick update: you are definitely pretty cool.

(To **PETER.***)* We gotta teach her the handshake.

SLIGHTLY. Peter, I'm very confused. I've never heard any lady people talk like this.

PETER. *(Deeply pleased and more in love with* **WENDY.***)* Then you better listen up. Everyone knows that a girl is worth twenty boys.

THE LOST BOYS. Some days twenty-five.

> (**WENDY** *likes Peter's response but now we hear a cannon in the distance.*)

TIGER LILY. Pirates are back.

PETER. Let's go underground boys.

TOOTLES.	**SLIGHTLY & CURLY.**
Get underground!	Underground we go!

WENDY. Why on earth would we go underground?

JOHN. Do you know what *lives* underground?

TOOTLES. *We* do!

CURLY. Our home is very dirty.

PETER. *(Correcting.)* It's very cozy.

CURLY. And very dirty.

SLIGHTLY. Come see!

TOOTLES. Yes come see, Wendy!

MICHAEL. Oh I'd love to.

WENDY. Well I suppose so.

JOHN. Is it quite safe down there, Mr. Pan?

PETER. No idea. LET'S GO!

> (*As the* **LOST BOYS** *open a secret door in a tree or stump or whatever you like and lead* **MICHAEL**, **JOHN**, *and* **WENDY** *underground.*)

WENDY. But why do these pirates chase you, Peter?

PETER. Well I mean, there's general evil madness, but also I cut off their captain's hand.

MICHAEL.	JOHN.	WENDY.
(Excited.)	*(Nervous.)*	*(Incredulous.)*
Really?!	His hand?	**That's the hand?!**

JOHN. Now why would you do a thing like that?

PETER. Because it was right *there*!

TIGER LILY. Then he threw it to my crocodile to eat.

PETER. Because he was right there!

*(At this **PETER** and all the **LOST BOYS** and their guests are underground. **TIGER LILY** and **WENDY** share a moment of mutual exhaustion with boys.)*

WENDY. So. Um. Are you the only girl in Neverland?

TIGER LILY. That's not a fairy, a mermaid or a crocodile. Jerome's got a girlfriend. She's nice.

WENDY. Ah. Well. I'm just so very glad you're here.

TIGER LILY. Hey. Same.

*(**TIGER** teachers her the handshake then **WENDY** descends but **TIGER LILY** stands guard, always vigilant.)*

Scene Three

(Later **CAPTAIN HOOK** *is enraged as* **SMEE** *and the* **PIRATES** *lead him to the same spot above the Lost Boys' lair.)*

CAPTAIN HOOK. If I don't have Pan on the hook by morning you're all *fired*, and I do mean *scorched* not *sacked*.

SMEE. *That's why we brought you here, sir.*

STARKEY. Yes, Captain! Don't kill us yet. We didn't get the boy, but we did get a clue!

JUKES. Tell 'em what we found, Smee!

NOODLER. Yeah tell him Smee! And also maybe mention to save the murder for the morning which would be amaaaaaazing.

CAPTAIN HOOK. What are they talking about, Smee.

SMEE. Well sir, very exciting actually, we did have a major discovery of note today.

CAPTAIN HOOK. What is it?!

SMEE. Oh no it's an actual note.

*(***SMEE*** reveals the Lost Boy's note!)*

Found it right here. A note to, what I believe to be, a Lost Boy. Judging by the adorableness of the message and the residual fairy dust.

*(***CAPTAIN HOOK*** snatches it and investigates.)*

CAPTAIN HOOK. A note to a Lost Boy.

JUKES. Tracks too. A passel of 'em.

STARKEY. *(Reveals a child's wooden sword.)* And a little wooden sword.

NOODLER. *(Reveals a doll made of sticks.)* And a rather terrifying sort of stick doll?

CAPTAIN HOOK. *It has to be them. Where are they?!*

SMEE. That's the puzzle sir, whoever was here just seemed to vanish into thin air.

> *(Revealing his genius idea to* **CAPTAIN HOOK** *with...)*

Or its opposite. What's the opposite of air?

> **PIRATES.** GROUND!
>
>> **SMEE.** What's opposite of up?
>>
>>> **PIRATES.** DOWN!
>>>
>>>> **SMEE.** Which got me thinking, we've searched the whole of the island but not –
>>>>
>>>> **CAPTAIN HOOK.** Under it.
>>>>
>>>> **SMEE.** Exactly, sir.

CAPTAIN HOOK. Underground. They live underground!

SMEE. Yes sir, and I think they actually live under *this* ground.

> *(***SMEE** *points at the very ground on which they stand.)*

Not so lost now are they.

CAPTAIN HOOK. Excellent work, Smee.

SMEE. Thank you, sir.

CAPTAIN HOOK. And the rest of you...are *not* going to presently die.

NOODLER.	**JUKES.**	**STARKEY.**
You don't know what this means to me!	Thank you, Captain.	What a guy. Love him.

CAPTAIN HOOK. Sharpen your swords, gentlemen. We strike tonight.

> *(***CAPTAIN HOOK*** exits with flourish and with* **SMEE**.*)*

ACT THREE

Scene One

Underground

(The underground home of Peter and the Lost Boys.)

(It's more of a playground than a house, way more fun than functional. They sing as they climb down.)

[MUSIC NO. 03 – FUN NEVERLAND SONG]

LOST BOYS.
>NEVERLAND! NEVERLAND, NEVERLAND!
>NEVERLAND, NEVERLAND – OY OY!
>ALL IS RIGHT THROUGH THE DAY AND NIGHT,
>WE SKIP, WE FLY, WE FIGHT FIGHT FIGHT IN
>NEVERLAND! NEVERLAND, NEVERLAND!
>NEVERLAND, NEVERLAND – OY OY!
>WE WAKE EACH DAY, TO A PIRATE FRAY
>WE RUN, WE ROAR, WE SLAY SLAY SLAY IN
>NEVERLAND! NEVERLAND, NEVERLAND!
>NEVERLAND, NEVERLAND – OY OY!
>THE FAIRIES GLOW, AND THE CANNONS BLOW
>AND THE MERMAIDS CREEP UNDER TIDES THAT FLOW
>SO WE SING, WE SCREAM, WE CROW CROW CROW IN

LOST BOYS.
> NEVERLAND! NEVERLAND, NEVERLAND!
> NEVERLAND, NEVERLAND – *NEVERLAND!*
>
> *(The **BOYS** descend into cheers and laughs and boasts of pride.)*

CURLY. WendyWendyWendy! This is our home and hideout and lair and WeLoveItDoYouLoveIt?

SLIGHTLY. And we've got a fireplace for fire, a swordplace for swords –

TOOTLES. And a pet bird and a pet lobster and pet skunk.

MICHAEL. Oh I rather like this place, Wendy.

CURLY. The little one likes it!

LOST BOYS. Yessssss!

SLIGHTLY. WaitWaitWait, do *you* like it, Wendy?

> *(**WENDY** is trying to be polite.)*

WENDY. Oh – well – It's very "Lost" and very "Boys."

TOOTLES.	**SLIGHTLY.**	**CURLY.**
Thank you!	Never thought about it that way.	**She gets it.**

WENDY. And does Tinkerbell live here as well?

> **CURLY.** Of course!
>
> > **TOOTLES.** Every home has a fairy.
> >
> > > **SLIGHTLY.** She lives in the jar.
>
> *(They point out a glass mason jar that serves as Tink's home.)*

WENDY. And does it have a lid?

JOHN. Mr. Pan, I do have a bit of a pressing concern.

PETER. What is it, John?

JOHN. This pirate captain person you mentioned?

PETER. Yes. Hook.

JOHN. Oh no, that's the whole concern. He sounds very scary and I'm wondering if you have a plan.

PETER. Of course we do, the plan is to fight him.

JOHN. Yes but – do you have a plan to *win*?

PETER. He's the villain, I'm the hero: of course I'll win.

LOST BOYS.	**MICHAEL.**
Of course he'll win!	Of course he'll win!

(**TINKERBELL'S BALL OF LIGHT** *flies into her glass home.* **WENDY** *sees this and surreptitiously turns it over trapping her like a caught firefly.*)

WENDY. Ah HAH.

JOHN. So you want to battle a vengeful tyrant and his vicious crew with a bunch of...children?

PETER. It's worked before. Good guy wins, bad guy loses, everyone cheers.

MICHAEL. Sounds right to me!

JOHN. Wendy, what do you think?

WENDY. I think...that I don't yet know how wise you are, Peter Pan, but you are definitely brave.

PETER. Well that's why I need *you*. For your lovely... wisdom.

(*They are both suddenly blushing at this...*)

(**TINKERBELL** *makes all kinds of racket at this from her glass jar.*)

SLIGHTLY. Wait! Perhaps Wendy doesn't want to be the mother because there is no father, but what if Wendy is our mother and *Peter* is our father!

> (**WENDY** and **PETER** are all about denying their flirtation. **TINKERBELL** is furious at this.)

TOOTLES.	**CURLY.**	**WENDY.**	**PETER.**
Ohh! Yes!	**That would work!**	No! What?	Oh that's not what I meant –

WENDY. I TOLD YOU. I will not be anyone's mother. But if you insist I will be your...Governor.

JOHN. You mean governess?

WENDY. I do not. You need someone in charge with some sense and strategy and...

> (Looking directly at **PETER**, a gift to him.)

And a bit of hope.

PETER. I like...

> (He means "you" but says...)

hope.

> (**PETER** smiles. They do like each other... Everyone notices. Beat.)

CURLY. (Whispering to **TOOTLES**.) Why are they looking like each is their favorite candy?

MICHAEL.	**TOOTLES.**	**SLIGHTLY.**
I don't know.	How strange.	**It's a mystery.**

> (This is broken by – Tinkerbell's jar falling over, and out pops the full sized **TINKERBELL**.)

TINKERBELL. BACK OFF, LADY, that is not your candy! You better SCATTER and FIND YOUR OWN PAN.

PETER. Calm down, Tink.

TINKERBELL. *I will not calm down. She trapped me like a BUG.*

> **WENDY.** You fly, you sting, these are *facts*.

>> **TINKERBELL.** I could have died in there!

>>> **WENDY.** I could have died in the stars!

>>>> **TINKERBELL.** You're trying to ruin everything!

>>>>> **WENDY.** You're doing a pretty good job of that on your own, you pinchy light up *pest*!

*(**TIGER LILY** jumps down into their fight.)*

TIGER LILY. ALRIGHT THAT'S ENOUGH. Don't you understand how utterly useless it is for girls to go against girls? The world's hard enough on us and then you turn on each other? Come on.

*(**WENDY** is ashamed. **TINKERBELL** is too.)*

TINKERBELL. Points were made.

WENDY. It's a...valid hypothesis.

TIGER LILY. Also the pirates are coming so let's focus on the real enemy here, shall we?

CURLY. The pirates are back?

WENDY. *Pirates?*

> **PETER.** Here we go.

>> **SLIGHTLY.** They're back!

>>> **JOHN.** What do we do?!

TIGER LILY. Stop giving away your location and put out that fire.

TOOTLES. Fire! Out! Hide!

TINKERBELL. *QUIET!*

[MUSIC NO. 04 – PIRATE SONG]

PIRATES. *(In the distance.)*
WE CROSS THE LAND, BOTH ROCK AND SAND
WE'LL FIGHT AND TAKE THE UPPERHAND
THEN DRAG YOU DOWN BELOW
THEN DRAG YOU DOWN BELOW

JOHN. *(Terrified.)* Those sound like real pirates!

MICHAEL. *(Excited.)* Those sound like real pirates!

TIGER LILY. Alright, everyone stay underground.

PETER. No. We go up the trees and attack from on high.

TIGER LILY. Sorry, your plan is to – what – jump on them and brawl?

PETER. That's exactly the plan.

TINKERBELL. GO, PETER!

TIGER LILY. Oh god he's going to make me save the day isn't he.

TINKERBELL. GO, PETER!

PETER. We'll go up and run the pirates off. Lost Boys, you stay below. Governor Wendy, you're in charge down here. When you hear my crow you know the fight's begun. Tink, Tiger, let's go,

TINKERBELL. GO, PETER!

*(**TINKERBELL** makes a mean face to **WENDY**, **TIGER LILY** opens a door to a secret passage.)*

TIGER LILY. Well don't just climb out and show them the entrance! At least take one of the secret passages.

LOST BOYS. There are secret passages?!

(*The* **LOST BOYS** *freeze as they hear.*)

PIRATES. (*Offstage.*)
YOU CAN'T ESCAPE US, THRASH OR SCRAPE US
BEST TO JOIN OR TRY AND TAKE US!
WATCH THE CANNONS BLOW
AND WATCH THE CANNONS BLOW

TIGER LILY. God I want vengeance, but I *really want to stop the singing.*

TINKERBELL. Right? Ugh. The worst.

TOOTLES.	**CURLY.**
I think it's catchy.	You don't like it?

SLIGHTLY. Just needs a bridge.

(**PETER** *climbs out of the underground home and* **TINKERBELL** *follows him.* **TIGER LILY** *and* **WENDY** *share a quick moment.*)

WENDY. Is fighting pirates a regular thing here?

TIGER LILY. Oh yeah. But somehow we don't die. Happy battle!

(**TIGER LILY** *follows* **PETER** *and climbs through a secret passage.*)

WENDY. *Wait, no, I don't battle, I'm more of a strategist!*

MICHAEL.	**JOHN.**
Can't I go with them?	I'm with you, Wendy.

(**CAPTAIN HOOK** *enters the Lost Boys' lair from a secret passage calm as a snake.*)

CAPTAIN HOOK. Hello, boys.

TOOTLES.	**SLIGHTLY.**	**CURLY.**	**JOHN.**
It's Hook!	He found us!	GOVERNOR **WENDY** WE HAVE A PROBLEM!	AHH!

> *(But before the* **LOST BOYS** *can reach for their swords,* **CAPTAIN HOOK** *points his sword at them which silences them.)*

CAPTAIN HOOK. Let's not make a commotion, shall we? These things tend to escalate so quickly in volume.

(To **WENDY.***)* You're new. What are you?

WENDY. My name is Wendy Moira Angela Darling, and I'm not afraid of you.

CAPTAIN HOOK. Oh good, I find the brave ones either overconfident or idiotic and, like a bird breaking its neck on a window, much more quickly dispatched because of it.

> *(Then we hear* **PETER** *crowing and attacking the pirates.)*

Speaking of which.

WENDY. Mr. Captain Hook. I know Peter cut off your hand, which must have been terribly uncomfortable, but there's no need to fight forever. There must be a peaceful accord to be had. Neverland needn't be a place of such mayhem when it is a place of such wonder.

CAPTAIN HOOK. Aw. Tie them up.

WENDY.	**SLIGHTLY.**	**TOOTLES.**	**CURLY.**
What?	No!	He'll kill us all, Wendy!	NoNoNoNo.

*(**CAPTAIN HOOK** tosses her...a white necktie just like her father's in Act One.)*

CAPTAIN HOOK. Can't have any distractions when I gut your leader in front of you so *tie. them. up.*

WENDY. This is...not a rope. It's my father's tie. Why do you have my father's tie?

CAPTAIN HOOK. Why indeed, my dear. Why indeed.

JOHN. What does he mean, Wendy?

MICHAEL. What does he want?

CAPTAIN HOOK. This isn't about what *I* want, it's what Pan wants. This is all his story, his rules, his world. Which means he's in charge.

CURLY. Of you?

CAPTAIN HOOK. Of us all.

*(**TINKERBELL** zooms in as a **BALL OF LIGHT** and **CAPTAIN HOOK** effortlessly snatches her. She wriggles and screams in his hand.)*

WENDY. Wait wait wait.

(Putting it all together, figuring it out. She points to the tie.)

Father's tie.

*(Points to **TINKERBELL**.)*

Mother's night light.

(Pointing all around.)

John's swords, Michael's crocodile, the stone that saved my life glows like radium, Why is our family all over Neverland?!

CAPTAIN HOOK. Because, Wendy Moira Angela Darling, you're Pan's favorite story.

And this is a world built from all his favorite things.

MICHAEL. But, Mister Captain Bad Guy if that's true, why are *you* here?

CAPTAIN HOOK. Every hero needs a villain, which makes me rather the Chief Executive of Neverland, emphasizing the "execute," of course.

> (**JOHN**'s *eyes light up.* **PETER** *and* **TIGER LILY** *re-enter the underground lair.*)

PETER. Get away from them, Hook!

CAPTAIN HOOK. Peter Pan. Were your ears burning, or is that your home?

> (*The* **LOST BOYS** *smell smoke.*)

SLIGHTLY. I smell dinner!

CURLY. That's not dinner, that's *us*.

TOOTLES. I'm hot, is anyone else hot?

JOHN.	**MICHAEL & CURLY.**	**SLIGHTLY.**	**WENDY.**
Are we on fire?!	Ahhh!	**So no dinner?**	This is not good!

TIGER LILY. Stop screaming, get to the surface, and RUN.

> (*But now the* **PIRATES** *flood in, entering in a rush, and continue the fight underground. The* **LOST BOYS** *and* **WENDY** *scamper to hide or escape the lair. The* **LOST BOYS** *are trying to exit, the* **PIRATES** *are trying to trap them. In the mayhem –*)

PETER. You want me, Hook, not them.

CAPTAIN HOOK. Oh, I want everything you have. Gotcha.

> (*As the* **LOST BOYS** *all try and exit,* **CAPTAIN HOOK** *effortlessly hooks* **JOHN**.)

JOHN. WENDY!

> **WENDY.** JOHN!
>
> > **TIGER LILY.** He's got the middle one!
> >
> > > **PETER.** Fight me, Hook, not the boy.
> > >
> > > > **MICHAEL.** THAT'S MY BROTHER, YOU LET HIM GO.

(**CAPTAIN HOOK** *casually releases* **JOHN** *with a shove.*)

CAPTAIN HOOK. Oh but he is free to go. Unless he'd like to join me. We're always looking for strapping young men with executive potential.

JOHN. Executive potential?

WENDY. John. No. Don't listen to him.

CAPTAIN HOOK. Yes listen to the ones who think you're too scared to amount to anything?

WENDY. THAT IS NOT TRUE. Peter stop this. If you're in charge of Neverland. Do something?!

PETER. What do you mean I'm in charge, no I'm not?

WENDY. He said this place is all in your control. That you built it from your favorite stories, which are mostly *my* stories in fact.

TIGER LILY. WHAT.

PETER. That's ridiculous. I didn't make Neverland and definitely not for me.

TIGER LILY. Well it's definitely not made for *me*.

CAPTAIN HOOK. Flying, fighting, no rules, no parents, no growing up, a subservient cohort of nitwits. Neverland is the dream of a greedy little boy.

PETER. *THAT'S NOT TRUE, HOOK. Neverland is a dream for everyone.*

WENDY. This isn't exactly the kind of place I would dream up.

SLIGHTLY. I would probably go with more unicorns.

TIGER LILY. I'd go with less colonial genocide.

CAPTAIN HOOK. How *is* your family, my dear, haven't seen them in a while.

TIGER LILY. *(She loses it when he mentions her family.)* Never will I, nor my family, nor this place be *yours*.

CAPTAIN HOOK. Let's test that theory. *(To his **CREW**.) Lock them in and light it up.*

> *(The **PIRATES** exit and lock them in. The sounds of fire crackling outside.)*

| **CURLY.** | **JOHN.** | **WENDY.** | **TOOTLES.** | **MICHAEL.** |
| NO! | Light us up?! | **Peter, do something!** | LET US OUT. | WENDY! |

WENDY. You built this place, you can change it!

PETER. I can't change anything!

CAPTAIN HOOK. Not until you admit why all this is here: You built Neverland, I want it, now we fight for it. If you dare.

> *(**PETER** stops. Face off across the expanse.)*

TIGER LILY. Peter.

> **WENDY.** Don't do this. Not when they've trapped us in here!

PETER. *(Turning back to fight* **CAPTAIN HOOK.***)* I do love a good dare.

WENDY. *Peter!*

TIGER LILY. *He's distracting you!*

CAPTAIN HOOK. Then have at thee, boy. Here and now.

*(***CAPTAIN HOOK** *and* **PETER** *fight again.* **WENDY** *and* **TIGER LILY** *take cover.)*

PETER. My pleasure, old man, I never get tired of winning.

CAPTAIN HOOK. And I never tire of forcing your hand.

PETER. Which one, I've got *two*.

*(***CAPTAIN HOOK** *rages at this and their battle intensifies.)*

CURLY. I'm thinking this is a good time for those secret passages.

WENDY. Take the others, we'll help Peter.

TIGER LILY. Then we'll get him to tell us what the hook is going on.

(The **LOST BOYS**, **JOHN**, *and* **MICHAEL** *run off through the secret passages.)*

CAPTAIN HOOK. You know the problem with staying young? You stay stupid.

*(***TIGER LILY** *spots the net and yells to* **WENDY**.*)*

TIGER LILY. Wendy! Here!

PETER. You know the problem with getting old? You think you know more than you do.

TIGER LILY. Tink, get ready!

CAPTAIN HOOK. I know how much easier it would be if we worked together. Your world, my plan. What a team we could –

TIGER LILY. NOW!

> (**TINKERBELL** *sprays* **CAPTAIN HOOK** *in the face with fairy dust and the* **GIRLS** *drop the net on* **CAPTAIN HOOK.** *He yelps, he's trapped, got fairy dust in his eyes.)*

CAPTAIN HOOK. Ahhhh. That is unsanctioned use of fairy dust! Come back here. PAN! We're not done. We finish this now!

WENDY. I think we just finished it. Can we go now?

PETER. Oh come on, I had him, it was just getting good.

WENDY. I retract the question. GO, PETER, NOW.

CAPTAIN HOOK. You need a yapping squad of girls to finish your fights? Not man enough to do it, yourself?!

PETER. Why be a man when you can stay a boy.

TIGER LILY. *Quiet.* Both of you.

(To **PETER.***)* You. Have a lot of explaining to do.

(To **CAPTAIN HOOK,** *unscrewing his hook.)* And you. You take and take and take. *NO MORE.*

(She takes the hook with her.)

Let's go.

> (**TIGER, WENDY,** *and* **TINKERBELL'S BALL OF LIGHT** *leave together.)*

CAPTAIN HOOK. Pan. Come back. Pan.

PETER. Tick tock, Hook.

> (**CAPTAIN HOOK** *struggles to free himself and catch* **PETER,** *but* **PETER** *flies off.)*

SMEE. Captain! The boy and his whole crew escaped and –

CAPTAIN HOOK. Smee.

SMEE. Yessir,

CAPTAIN HOOK. I'm aware.

(**SMEE** *disentangles* **CAPTAIN HOOK**, *seeing his hookless hand, gasps. Pulls out an extra, less impressive hook, and attaches it.*)

Destroy it.

*(But suddenly, who enters...but **JOHN**.)*

JOHN. Mr. Captain Hook? About the um...open executive position?

(**CAPTAIN HOOK** *and* **SMEE** *glare...* **JOHN** *does the same "intimidating stance" from Act One.* **CAPTAIN HOOK** *likes the leverage he just got and grins.*)

CAPTAIN HOOK. Welcome aboard, son.

(As we transition swiftly to...)

A Cliff Above the Forest

(Stark lighting cut to **PETER, TIGER LILY, WENDY, MICHAEL, TINKERBELL,** *and the* **LOST BOYS** *panting from running. They turn to watch from afar as the fire consuming their home grows and grows.)*

TOOTLES. The one safe place we had in Neverland is gone.

CURLY. Wait, did we just win or lose?

SLIGHTLY. What are we gonna do now Peter?

PETER. I'll fix it, I promise. You can always count on me.

TIGER LILY. Can we? You better tell me Hook was wrong and you're not causing all this.

PETER. Of course I'm not! You believe Hook over me? Come on, boys. And two girls. And a fairy. And Jerome and his girlfriend. Don't worry. I will find us a new home, and keep us together, and never stop fighting for Neverland.

TINKERBELL. For Neverland.

MICHAEL & LOST BOYS. For Neverland!

*(**TIGER LILY** tosses Hook's hook to the ground.)*

TIGER LILY. For Neverland.

WENDY. For Neverland.

Wait. Where's John?

(Blackout.)

Intermission

ACT FOUR

Scene One

The Seacave

*(A gorgeous, glittering cave. An underground lake casts curvy blue light on the walls and ceiling. This is a safe haven from the pirates. Perhaps a **MERMAID** makes an appearance before...)*

*(***PETER**, **TIGER LILY**, **WENDY**, **JOHN**, **MICHAEL**, **TINKERBELL**, *and the* **LOST BOYS** *run in and regroup.* **WENDY** *is writing/sketching in her notebook constantly.)*

PETER. In in in, everyone – in here we're safe and it's even better than the underground home because there's only one entrance, it's hidden from the outside, not on any map, it's perfect.

SLIGHTLY. And damp.

   CURLY. It *is* a little moist.

      TOOTLES. And smells like fish secrets.

         SLIGHTLY. What are fish –?

            TOOTLES. *Shhhhhhhhh.*

(Investigating one of many glass-like disks or balls on the cave floor.)

WENDY. How beautiful! It's some transparent sort of sea glass?

> (**MICHAEL** *takes two and puts them against his eyes like goggles and* **WENDY** *gathers some sea glass specimens in her bag.*)

MICHAEL. Or sea *glasses*!

TOOTLES.   **SLIGHTLY.**   **CURLY.**
Oooohhhhhhh.   He's got glasses!   I get it!

> (*The* **LOST BOYS** *imitate* **MICHAEL** *playing with the sea glass.*)

TINKERBELL. PeterPeterPeter, okay, you know I think you're the absolute best, but we can't stay here, Peter. This is where the mermaids live. The *mermaids*.

PETER. Oh come on, the mermaids love me, it'll be fine.

WENDY. Real mermaids?

MICHAEL. Oh, I think I'd like to see one of those.

LOST BOYS. NO YOU DON'T.

TINKERBELL. Not when they drag children underwater for fun.

MICHAEL. This place is one fascinating hazard after the next.

WENDY. I can't stay here, Peter, not when John is out there alone with Hook. We have to go and get him back!

PETER. I will rescue him, don't worry, I just need the right moment to strike Hook down for good.

TIGER LILY. The right moment to make this a story all about *you* again?

PETER. OK, come on. Don't listen to Hook, This place isn't mine, I didn't make it, I'm just trying to save the day!

TIGER LILY. Which means all of Neverland is *one big playground built just for you!*

PETER. Tiger, calm down.

TIGER LILY. *Would you calm down if someone put your family in their stories just to slaughter!*

PETER. *I didn't do that, I just never wanted to grow up!*

When I was small, I heard my first fairy story, and I thought "where do stories go when they're over? Because stories never grow up, and the people in them never grow up, you just start them over when you want another adventure and I always want another adventure *so take me to the story place, fairy people!"* And then she did.

   TINKERBELL. And then I did.

      PETER. And here I was.

         TINKERBELL. And here we are.

PETER. And she said "this is Neverland" and I said "sure," and it was perfect but...also empty. So I went for more stories to fill it up: heroic adventure and fantastic animals and voyages on pirate ships and –

TIGER LILY. People like mine run off their land by people like yours.

PETER. *No*, by people like Hook!

TIGER LILY. *Which means you brought Hook here because you care more about a good fight than you care about us.* Stories are powerful, Peter. Neverland could have been a place of peace and friendship and you made it a place of boys and battle and we all suffer.

PETER. No, we beat them every time! It's not my fault if it's also fun.

TIGER LILY. *This isn't fun for everyone.* We're the pieces, you're the player. I'm the unflinching sidekick. They're the ones you get to boss around. And Tinkerbell is obviously here so you don't have to exist a moment without constant adoration.

TINKERBELL. *Hey.*

(*To* **PETER.**) Don't listen, you're awesome.

TIGER LILY. *You brought Hook and pirates and everything you need for your story but what about me?!* You brought my family just to take them *away?!* No. I'm done. I'll finish this on my own.

PETER. (*Starting to get mad.*) If you want to be finished I'm sure Hook can see to that.

TIGER LILY. Exactly. You think like him, you act like him, which means, Peter Pan, you are real close to *being* him.

PETER. OK ENOUGH JUST STOP IT, you can't do this on your own!

TIGER LILY. YES. I. CAN. Hook's not in between me and freedom. YOU ARE.

(**TIGER LILY** *goes to leave.*)

WENDY. Wait, no. Please don't go. You're the smartest one of them all. What can I do?

TIGER LILY. Leave. Because I'm defeating him one way or another.

MICHAEL. Defeat who?

WENDY. Hook or Peter?

TIGER LILY. (*Pointedly to* **PETER.**) I haven't decided.

Let's go Jerome.

(*A growl echoes from the cave as* **TIGER LILY** *runs off.*)

PETER. Don't listen to her, boys.

WENDY. But Peter, she's right. No one's free if Neverland is just one fight after the next. And now the only one who knows what to do has abandoned us, the mermaids want us drowned, your home was burned to ash, and those pirates *took my brother*! *This is no story, this danger is real.*

> (**TINKERBELL** *points to a* **MERMAID** *reaching up from the water or from behind a rock and trying to grab* **MICHAEL**'s *foot.*)

TINKERBELL. Mermaid.

WENDY & MICHAEL.	**CURLY.**	**TOOTLES.**
Ah!	Watch out!	*Nope.*

SLIGHTLY. They are so mean.

> (**MICHAEL** *jumps away and runs to* **WENDY** *who protects him.*)

PETER. Wendy.

WENDY. No, that's it. Michael, we're getting John and we're going home.

PETER. Home? No. You can't leave.

WENDY. I will do whatever is necessary to protect my family from harm. And right now that's you.

TINKERBELL.	**CURLY.**	**TOOTLES.**	**SLIGHTLY.**
(*Like "ohh snap."*) Ohhhhhhhhhhhh.	Ouch.	Yikes.	Burn.

PETER. But Wendy if you leave now, if you leave Neverland, you'll grow up and that means you won't have…

> (*He wants to say "me" but instead says.*)

Adventure. That is not who you are.

WENDY. Everyone seems to decide who I am except for me. You brought me here to be some sort of mother?!

PETER. And then you *showed me* I was wrong! You're an explorer of stars, sticker of shadows, you know things and stand up for yourself, you won't settle, you won't let people down, you're a governor and a scientist and a teller of stories and you dream the very best dreams I've ever seen.

> *(That was his declaration of love, though he'd never call it that. She knows.)*

WENDY. Thank you. But you can't live only in a world of dreams, Peter. You can't.

> *(**WENDY** goes to comfort **PETER** with a touch, he flinches. **PETER** is obviously upset but won't show it.)*

PETER. Then I obviously should have never brought you here. You wanna leave? Fine. I can save you from everything else, but I can't save you from a dumb idea.

TINKERBELL.	**CURLY.**	**TOOTLES.**	**SLIGHTLY.**
(Like "ohh snap.") Ohhhhhhhhhhhh.	Ouch.	Yikes.	Burn.

WENDY. Peter...

PETER. You know I went home once, and you know what I found? *My window was locked and another boy was in my bed because my mother had forgotten all about me.* So maybe *you* don't need Neverland but it is all I have. You wanna go? Go. Fight Hook yourself, get your brother, and good riddance.

WENDY. *FINE.*

> **TOOTLES.** WAIT!
>
> > **PETER.** What?
> >
> > > *(The **LOST BOYS** run up and whisper to **WENDY**.)*

WENDY. They'd like to come too.

SLIGHTLY. If we may, Peter.

CURLY. If you think we should.

PETER. I think you're a fool and I don't care what you do.

WENDY. They're not fools to want a real family.

PETER. They're fools to think that a real family will give them the freedom they have here.

> **WENDY.** Not everyone's freedom looks the same, Peter.
>
>> **PETER.** Mine certainly doesn't look like yours.
>>
>>> **WENDY.** How do you know?

PETER. *Because you're not talking about a family, you're talking about growing up, and no one will make me do something so terrible as that.*

WENDY. Yes, well Marie Curie grew up and she turned out just fine.

TINKERBELL. WHO IS MARIE CURIE, IS SHE A GIRL, IS SHE COMING HERE?! IS SHE FRENCH?

> **WENDY.** SHE'S POLISH
>
>> **TINKERBELL.** I DIDN'T KNOW THAT, THAT'S FASCINATING.

PETER. It's not, it's idiotic, and so is every one of you who wants to leave this place, grow up and lose everything worth living for, because THAT I will not do!

WENDY. THEN YOU'LL MISS YOUR WHOLE LIFE AND EVERYONE ELSE'S. You're not refusing to grow up, you're refusing to care about anyone but yourself. Tiger Lily is right again. If you keep pushing people away, and listening only to stories you want to hear, *you're not going to beat Captain Hook, you're going to **become** him.*

WENDY. *(To everyone else.)* Let's go, boys. We'll be our own heroes.

MICHAEL. Goodbye then. Peter. It was ever so much fun.

CURLY. Bye Peter.

SLIGHTLY. See you…never, I guess.

TOOTLES. Tootles.

> (**WENDY** *takes out the glowing rock that* **PETER** *gave her. She gives it back to him. He turns away.*)

TINKERBELL. Yeah, good riddance, WendyThing!

> (**WENDY**, **MICHAEL**, *and the* **LOST BOYS** *exit the cave.*)

Fiiiiinally. Just us. How it allllll started.

> (**PETER** *doesn't respond.*)

Look, no one wants her out of here more than I do, but…you're really going to let them battle Hook without you?

PETER. She stormed off, not me. They don't want a hero, they don't like Neverland, *good luck then.*

TINKERBELL. RightYesTooootallyGetThat but I mean… this just doesn't sound very "Peter Pan" to me.

  PETER. (Well As Peter Actual Pan, I really think it does.)

    TINKERBELL. Well I really think you're being a stubborn sad pants that can't possibly want to abandon your friends to your biggest nemesis!

      PETER. THEN YOU CAN GO TOO. I don't need ANY OF YOU, NONE OF YOU so for ONCE IN YOUR LIFE, TINK, JUST LEAVE ME ALONE.

*(**TINKERBELL** is shocked, hurt, pissed.)*

TINKERBELL. Just remember, Peter Pan: *I* didn't leave, *you* pushed.

*(**TINKERBELL** exits with sass and a spiteful fling of fairy dust.)*

*(**PETER** is alone.)*

*(Except for his **SHADOW** who wants to go after **WENDY** and the **LOST BOYS**.)*

PETER. *(To his **SHADOW**.)* Nonono. Adventures are much better on your own.

Obviously. Everyone knows that.

Because it's very obvious.

All you need is yourself and your shadow.

*(Peter's **SHADOW** is unconvinced, then sees a **MERMAID** approaching.)*

*(A **MERMAID**'s hand tries to grab **PETER**'s leg.)*

WOULD YOU STOP. Not everyone is part fish.

*(The **MERMAID** retreats. Then someone clears their throat in the darkness.)*

HOOK. Mr. Pan. Alone. What a thing.

*(**HOOK** emerges. **PETER** doesn't even flinch. He's over it. Doesn't care.)*

PETER. Wow. Yeah. You got me. Okay, what are we doing here? Swords, knives, you're gonna start calling me "insipid little boy"? I don't really care just – "have at thee," sure, whatever. Can we move it along here?

(**HOOK** *is a bit disarmed by* **PETER**'s *lackluster approach.*)

HOOK. I'm going to be honest this is a bit more casual than I expected, and that does diminish the joy of this particular brand of vengeance.

PETER. It doesn't matter, Hook. We do this every day. Do what you want. I don't care.

HOOK. Well I do. One of us is going to win this.

PETER. You, me, a mermaid, I'm gonna go.

(**HOOK** *whips out his sword and points it at* **PETER**'s *chest.*)

HOOK. You're not going anywhere.

(**PETER** *rages at him, grabs his sword, really goes for him during this.*)

PETER. *Then do it, Hook. You want to slice me up so badly, you want to end me, then do it. I'll fight you. I'd love to. I am always ready, and I always get away, and we do this over and over and WHY. WHY.*

(**HOOK** *again is startled by this very different* **PETER PAN**.)

HOOK. Because. You and I are perfect enemies.

PETER. Because we hate each other.

HOOK. No. Because we *understand each other.* Aren't we both some version of the boy who rejected his parents for the life of a misfit? This *is* yours isn't it?

(**HOOK** *reveals that note from before.* **PETER** *snatches it protectively, it's his.*)

I have one too, you know. "Be good," my mother wrote to me as a boy. "No" I wrote back. I don't know why I keep it but, like you, I do.

PETER. Stop it, Hook. Stop pretending you know anything about me.

HOOK. Oh please you are not that much of a mystery. "I'm Peter Pan, follow me, I can't be alone even though I push everyone away. Crow! Fight! Fly! Repeat!"

PETER. Well you're just as obvious. "I'm a big scary pirate and a little boy hurt me and I want to hurt him back! Swords out! Wig on! Sing the stupid song!"

HOOK. I know, I detest that song.

PETER. Then what are we doing? Every day we battle, every day I escape, what's the point?

HOOK. You really don't know, do you? The *point*...is that stories are powerful and somehow *you* control them. Which subsequently, and of most interest to yours truly, means that you control the minds of every young dreamer because they dream of *you*. The more they dream the stronger you are, the stronger you are the more they want to *be* you, the more they want to *be* you the more control you have, and to *control the dreams of the world is to control everything in it.*

PETER. That's not what I'm doing, Neverland is just for fun, I'm just doing what I want to do.

HOOK. Then you should keep having fun...and give Neverland to me.

PETER. I can't give you something that's not mine.

   HOOK. This whole place runs on your desires!

      PETER. How can I control something I don't know I'm controlling?!

         HOOK. *Because you don't care about anything but yourself!*

           PETER. That's not true!

              HOOK. I said it as a compliment!

HOOK. I don't want to change that. I want to work together.

All this time I've been fighting *for* something, and you've just been...fighting. But if we combine our methods we can do something real, real power...**power even *beyond* Neverland**. We don't have to beat each other to win everything. You can play all you want, and I can rule as I please... And the power of all those little minds will be...redirected.

PETER. Redirected?

HOOK. When the hero changes, the story changes, and... so does the future.

PETER. You're...you're serious.

HOOK. If you can make children dream of being Hook instead of Pan...well that's a very different world isn't it. Have you even considered how much more fun it is to be me? No cares, no guilt, no allegiance, no need to be anyone's hero but my own? You should try it.

> (**HOOK** *offers* **PETER** *his sword. After a moment* **PETER** *takes it, tries it, likes it.*)

> (*Just then* **TINKERBELL** *re-enters.*)

TINKERBELL. PETER, it's a trap! Get away from him!

   PETER. TINK, I – I –

      TINKERBELL. His pirates were waiting for us at the mouth of the cave and took everyone!

HOOK. Oh yes, that was the plan. Plant the seeds of doubt, reap the fields of distrust. Don't have to kidnap anyone if they walk out on their own. At this moment the crew is hauling them back to the ship for, let's just say, disembarkation.

TINKERBELL. *(To* **HOOK**.*) You do not get to make my friends and one Wendy walk the plank!* What's wrong with you Peter? What are you waiting for?!

PETER. You left, they all left.

> **TINKERBELL.** Because you pushed them away! Now go after them!
>
>> **HOOK.** Do you shut her up or should I?
>>
>>> **TINKERBELL.** I'M A OPINIONATED FAIRY, I NEVER SHUT UP!
>>>
>>> *(***TINKERBELL** *runs full on at* **HOOK**.*)*
>>>
>>> *(***HOOK** *is unprepared for* **TINKERBELL***'s power and fervor.)*

PETER. TINK, NO. HOOK, DON'T!

> *(Then* **HOOK** *rips her wing with his hook. She falls.* **PETER** *grabs his sword and challenges* **HOOK**. **HOOK** *doesn't fight* **PETER**. *Calmly starts walking away.)*

HOOK. Sorry, old friend.

Looks like your mum was wrong. You *are* alone.

Battle, my ship, midnight? Good.

> *(***HOOK** *takes back his sword and is gone.)*
>
> *(***TINKERBELL** *is badly injured. Her light is fading, she falters.)*

PETER. NoNoNo. Tink. It's gonna be okay.

TINKERBELL. Is it? What's a fairy without wings?

PETER. You'll be fine, Tink. I'll fix this. Somehow.

TINKERBELL. *(Accusing him.)* What happened to you? To my…

TINKERBELL. *(Getting weak.)* My Peter...

> *(Her light gets dimmer. She winces, she's fainting.)*

PETER. Tink. Nonono I need you to be okay.

TINKERBELL. And we need you to believe.

> **PETER.** Believe what?!
>
> > **TINKERBELL.** *That Neverland needs more than one kind of hero.* No one saves the day alone, Peter. No one –

(Her light is almost gone, she passes out.)

PETER. SOMEBODY. HELP.

> *(Nothing. No response.)*

MERMAIDS, CROCODILES, ANYONE, COME ON.

Nonono, Tink, I can't do this without you, I need you! TINK.

> *(He sees the glowing rock that **WENDY** just returned to him. Grabs it.)*

Please tell me what to do. You know everything, what do I do to save her?!

> *(He listens to the rock which glows bright in his hand.)*

What do you mean...there *are* dreamers out there? Right now? Listening to...*me*?

> *(A revelation of what **TINKERBELL** just said.)*

"No one saves the day alone." Yes. *Yes.*

> *(So sad, so vulnerable. **PETER** expresses this almost as a prayer...)*

If you're out there, dreamers, anyone, please… I need your help, she's my…my family, and you have to help me save her, because I will do anything to save her, because what is Peter Pan without Tinkerbell, and what is life without the people you love?!

(Shocked that he just said that.) And we might not be able to save her, but if you – I don't know – let me know you're out there, at least we'll know we're not alone. And she always really liked applause.

> *(**PETER** hears the audience's applause and cheers almost from afar. He is overwhelmed with gratitude and sincere awe.)*

Yes, clap, thank you, yes, it's working, clap, stomp, whatever you can. Don't be silent, don't sit still. Keep going! Please believe, please, please believe…!

> *(Soon our dear **TINKERBELL** shines bright as a bulb again. She stands!)*

TINKERBELL. Peter?

> *(But instead of speaking a word **PETER** runs to **TINKERBELL** and hugs her.)*

> *(This is the first time he's ever touched someone on purpose. In this hug are all the things he can't say to her: I love you, thank you, I'm sorry.)*

PETER. You and me. Forever.

TINKERBELL. You and me, Peter Pan. Forever.

> *(**TINKERBELL** might wink at the audience right before… Blackout.)*

ACT FIVE

Scene One

Pirate Ship

(On the deck of Captain Hook's pirate ship. Skull and Crossbones fly.)

*(**CAPTAIN HOOK** is getting ready for his big battle like most would get ready for a nice dinner. He tries on different hooks. **PIRATES** roam the deck on red alert. They are sure Pan is coming – they don't know when. **HOOK** paces near a covered birdcage...)*

SMEE. Here we are Captain. At the beginning of another battle together. I do so love these quiet moments just us, sir. And may I say how honored I am to have played a small role in getting us to this point. It's your vision, of course, but it makes me prouder than I can say to have helped you live your dreams...and steal the dreams of others.

HOOK. Smee.

SMEE. Yessir.

HOOK. Time to stop talking.

SMEE. Of course sir.

HOOK. *(Calling.)* Bring out the new recruit!

*(**JUKES** enters with **JOHN** in his new/old pirate gear, he's really trying to play the part but he's terrified. **JUKES** is his mentor. **SMEE** doesn't like **JOHN** one bit.)*

JUKES. Here he is, Captain. Been giving the new guy a bit of a pirate run down. Covered the basics: sword fighting, ale guzzling, and a bit of meteorology, always gotta watch the skies at sea.

JOHN. Yes, Mister Jukes has been very helpful.

*(To **JUKES**.)* Thank you very much indeed, sir.

JUKES. *(Over the top pirate voice.)* Argh, matey!

JOHN. *(Imitating him with an over the top pirate voice.)* Argh, matey!

JUKES. Kidding, we don't really say it like that. One pirate says "arghh" and everyone thinks we all do it.

JOHN. Oh dear, my apologies.

JUKES. No sweat, you're learning.

*(To **HOOK**.)* Good kid.

*(To **JOHN**.)* Don't die.

*(**JUKES** leaves them, **JOHN** gulps.)*

HOOK. There you have it Mr. Darling, you're fitting right in. I'd wager you'll give Mr. Smee a run for his money one day.

*(Now **SMEE** really hates **JOHN**.)*

JOHN. Oh no, Mr. Smee, I would never step on your toes.

SMEE. I don't have toes.

JOHN. Oh my.

HOOK. Take it in, gentlemen. What always mesmerizes about this time of night is the sheer power of children dreaming stupid little stories in their stupid little heads. I can feel it, can't you?

SMEE. Like an itch I can't reach, sir.

JOHN. Yes, me too. Very itchy.

HOOK. So many of them curled up, lids shut, feeding this place with their useless little thoughts. They dream of Neverland. They dream of Pan. Dreams of him are adventures; but dreams of me are nightmares. I really can't see why.

> *(He lifts the sheet off of the birdcage and we see that* **WENDY** *and* **TIGER LILY** *are inside, gagged.* **JOHN** *gasps.)*

JOHN. *Wendy?!*

HOOK. Then again, nightmares can scar the mind for life and I do so love to *stick around*.

SMEE. I dunno, Captain. I don't think the young one's up to the task. He's too scared to be a real pirate.

JOHN. *I am not scared, I'm a formidable menace and very comfortable with financial warfare, I mean general warfare, I mean pirate effrontery!*

SMEE. *Then prove it.* How do *you* think we should dispatch the captives?

HOOK. Yes, Mr. Darling. Would you like to drown them or join them?

JOHN. ...I...

> *(***HOOK*** ungags ***WENDY***'s mouth.* ***SMEE*** *ungags ***TIGER LILY***.)*

WENDY. John, what are you doing with this madman.

TIGER LILY. How could you!

HOOK. John knows power when he sees it, which is why he's smarter than all of you.

JOHN. Yes, but Captain –

HOOK. KILL OR DIE, JOHN, THOSE ARE YOUR OPTIONS.

(**JOHN** *is too scared to move.*)

WENDY. John, listen to me. You are better than this.

HOOK. I think we can all agree that it's better outside the cage than in. Speaking of which, I did have a nice long talk with your friend Peter –

SMEE. *(Betrayed.)* With Pan without me?

WENDY. *What did you do to him.*

HOOK. Just chatted about how much we have in common.

SMEE. *With Pan without me?*

HOOK. Especially after I ripped the wings off his little fairy thing and he really started to really come around to my ideas.

TIGER LILY.	**WENDY.**
What happened to Tinkerbell?	Is she alright?

SMEE. Captain, I really feel a breach of trust in our working relationship –

WENDY. *John, you've got to get us out of here!*

HOOK. NOT GOING TO HAPPEN. You're the bait, Pan's the fool, without his fairy dust I'll slay him in seconds, and we're all done before dawn.

TIGER LILY. It's a very old plot, Hook, I thought you could do better.

HOOK. Young people always think old ideas are useless when in truth they are highly confirmed strategies.

WENDY. I dare you to doubt us.

TIGER LILY. Yeah Hook. I dare you.

HOOK. Chilling. Time for drowning.

> **SMEE.** Yessir, of course sir.

>> **HOOK.** *Bring out the rest of the brats.*

>> (**PIRATES** *bring out another cage of the rest of* **LOST BOYS** *and* **MICHAEL**.)

MICHAEL.	**CURLY.**	**WENDY.**	**TOOTLES.**	**SLIGHTLY.**
Wendy!	Tiger!	Michael!	This isn't fun anymore!	Where is Peter!

SMEE. Silence, you Tiny Problems!

HOOK. John, my boy, have you decided what to do with our captives?

WENDY.	**TIGER LILY.**	**MICHAEL.**	**SLIGHTLY.**	**CURLY.**
JOHN!	Come on!	What are you doing?	Yikes.	Not a good look.

JOHN. Um. I think – perhaps – we could – um – scold them – heartily of course – and no dessert?

HOOK. Yeah see I was thinking the plank.

SMEE. I AGREE WITH THE CAPTAIN BECAUSE WE'RE VERY CLOSE AND WORK SO WELL TOGETHER.

> **WENDY.** The plank?!

>> **MICHAEL.** There's a plank?!

>>> **SMEE.** Yes there's a plank, what kind of pirates do you think we are.

MICHAEL.	**SLIGHTLY.**	**CURLY.**	**TOOTLES.**
No!	You can't do this!	Where's Peter?	**Help!**

WENDY. JOHN, YOU HAVE TO DO SOMETHING.

HOOK. You see, John, *now* they need you. When you're holding the sword, when their lives are in your hands, *now* they respect you. Don't you feel the difference when you're feared instead of loved?

> (*The* **PIRATES** *cackle at this.* **SMEE** *maybe laughs too hard.*)

SMEE. GOOD ONE, CAPTAIN, LOVE HIM, TOTALLY DEVOTED AND UTTERLY TERRIFIED.

MICHAEL. Please John. This is not who you are!

JOHN. *Maybe it's who I want to be!*

MICHAEL. It's not, it's who Father wants you to be!

WENDY. I know you want to be brave and mighty, John, but don't you see you already are. You are smart, and cautious, and kind and those things make you stronger than people twice your size, because they make you *good*.

HOOK. Good and *dead*, that's how we do it on the Jolly Roger!

STARKY.	**NOODLER.**	**JUKES.**	**SMEE.**
Said it before, love dead.	**Slay! All! Day!**	Whee!	GENIUS, CAPTAIN.

JOHN. But I'm *not good! Never once has Father said I was good at anything, and you and Michael think I'm a coward, and Mother wishes she never had a son as disappointing as I.*

> (*Everyone feels terrible for* **JOHN**. *Even the* **PIRATES**, *who honestly feel his pain.*)

STARKEY. Been there, matey.

TOOTLES.	**JUKES.**	**CURLY.**	**SLIGHTLY.**
Me too.	Oh yeah.	Me too.	Absolutely.

NOODLER. All of middle school.

WENDY. Mother and Father don't understand *me* either, John, but that doesn't mean we change *for them*, it means we *change* them.

HOOK. *A reckless damsel can't change a thing, and neither can her mouse-hearted little brother!*

MICHAEL. *(With full force.) You leave my family alone! They came to Neverland because they are the bravest, smartest and strongest people you've ever crossed and they have all of us at their back!*

SMEE. You may have their back but we have the swords.

JOHN. Well I have one too. And I just realized that I have something you don't.

NOODLER. Is it love?

    STARKEY. See that's what *I* thought.

    JUKES. I bet it's insurance.

JOHN. I have something more than myself to fight for: a family that loves me as I am.

STARKY.	**NOODLER.**	**JUKES.**
Awww.	Actually quite touching.	**You were right, it was love.**

HOOK. *(Re:* **JOHN.***)* Oh fine, kill that one too.

JUKES. *(To* **JOHN.***)* Come on, man, the one thing I said was don't die.

    (Now they all take **HOOK** *on, being brave together, standing up to him.)*

WENDY. John's right. We know why we're fighting.

MICHAEL. Which means *we* have the courage!

JOHN. Because we have each other

> **TIGER LILY.** And you have nothing but hate, *old man*.
>
> > **CURLY.** It's not the croc you fear, Hook.
> >
> > > **TOOTLES.** *It's the clock.*
> > >
> > > > **SLIGHTLY.** Because you know it's *running out for you.*
> > > >
> > > > > **WENDY.** *But **we** have all the time in the world.*
> > > > >
> > > > > > **TIGER LILY.** Because it's *our world to save.*
> > > > > >
> > > > > > > **JOHN.** *And we'll do it, together.*
> > > > > > >
> > > > > > > > **LOST BOYS.**
> > > > > > > > *(Cheering **JOHN**.)* Yeah!

(Suddenly the lights go out. Startled reactions from all.)

CURLY. What's going on?

> **PIRATES.** The lights!
>
> > **WENDY.** Are you alright, boys?
> >
> > > **SLIGHTLY.** I can't see!
> > >
> > > > **PIRATES.** Me neither!
> > > >
> > > > > **MICHAEL & JOHN.** Wendy?
> > > > >
> > > > > > **TIGER LILY.** Stay calm!
> > > > > >
> > > > > > > **STARKEY.** A ghost!
> > > > > > >
> > > > > > > > **NOODLER.** A spirit!
> > > > > > > >
> > > > > > > > > **JUKES.** The ship's bewitched!

SMEE. It's the girls. Never was luck on a pirate ship with women aboard.

WENDY & TIGER LILY. OH COME ON.

NOODLER. Lights!

   HOOK. Candles!

      STARKEY. Who's got the flame?

         JUKES. We need light!

         (**PETER PAN** *snaps his fingers and* **TINKERBELL'S BALL OF LIGHT** *illuminates his face.* **PETER** *whistles and waves.*)

         (**PETER'S SHADOW** *waving at them all too.*)

PETER. I've got one.

LOST BOYS. Peter!

HOOK. PAN.

JUKES.	**WENDY.**	**TIGER.**	**PIRATES.**	**BOYS.**
There he is!	It's a trap!	He's using us as bait!	Got him now!	Help us!

(*Suddenly* **TINKERBELL'S LIGHT** *swirls around the stage and unlocks all the cages, setting the* **LOST BOYS, WENDY,** *and* **TIGER LILY** *free.*)

SMEE. He's got his fairy back, Captain!

PETER. I do and she's very mad at you. Everybody out!

(*The* **CAPTIVES** *realize the locks are open thanks to* **TINKERBELL** *and burst free.*)

WENDY.	**TIGER LILY.**	**MICHAEL.**	**JOHN.**	**LOST BOYS.**
GO GO!	**HURRY!**	I'm free!	Oh good lord.	RUN! RUN!

STARKEY. They're out!

JUKES. They're loose, Captain!

HOOK. THEN FIGHT THEM!

>*(The fight's begun!* **PIRATES** *vs* **LOST BOYS** *and* **STRONG GIRLS**. *There are no guns, only swords. From across the fray...)*

>*(**JOHN** runs to **WENDY** and hugs her.)*

JOHN. I'm so sorry, Wendy! I'm so sorry!

WENDY. It's alright. For now just protect your brother, I'll get mad at you later.

JOHN. That's fair. *Michael!*

>*(**JOHN** and **MICHAEL** work together to kick some pirate butt. The **PIRATES** corner the **LOST BOYS** until –)*

>*(**TINKERBELL** emerges in full with a glitter/fairy dust explosion that stuns and disables the **PIRATES**!)*

TINKERBELL. *(To the* **PIRATES**.*)* How's that for *fairyworks?!*

JUKES.	**NOODLER.**	**STARKEY.**
I'm allergic to fairy dust!	It's in my eyes!	It's so beautiful and terrible!

TIGER LILY. Get them in the cages!

>*(**TIGER LILY**, **WENDY**, and **TINKERBELL** shove **PIRATES** into their own cages. Girls win!)*

WENDY. That was so satisfying. Young women united in force!

TINKERBELL. Oh you just say "girl power."

TIGER LILY. It's just "girl power."

WENDY. Oh yeah that's better. Girl Power!

(**PETER** *runs up to* **TIGER LILY**.)

PETER. Tiger, I'm sorry, I was wrong. I didn't see it before, but Neverland isn't safe or fun or free for anyone but me. But it shouldn't be that way. Help me change it. We beat Hook, we build a *new* Neverland from *new* stories.

TIGER LILY. And the *old*. My people have been telling stories for thousands of years. We start with them.

PETER. Yes! Though I know it won't bring your family back.

TIGER LILY. It might. Telling people's stories is the closest thing anyone gets to bringing them back.

Alright Pan. Let's do this...*together.*

PETER. Together.

WENDY. Together.

TINKERBELL. Together!

PETER. Thank you. All of you. Hook is too strong. I need your ideas, your advice, I can't beat him alone.

WENDY. (*A "Eureka!" moment.*) *My advice! That's it! We can use my advice!*

(*She pulls out the magnifying glass from her bag.*)

Tink! I'm gonna need some serious sparkle. Can you do it?

TINKERBELL. Anytime, anywhere.

WENDY. If Tink does her magic, Tiger gets her crocodile, and I bring the science, I think we can stop him.

TIGER LILY. On it.

PETER. But what do I do?

WENDY. Crow.

> *(The **GIRLS** scatter to prepare their plan.)*

> *(Just then, **HOOK** re-emerges in all his glory.)*

HOOK. Proud and insolent youth, prepare thyself.

PETER. Sinister old man, I guess you better have at thee.

> *(**PETER** crows and **HOOK** and **PETER** start their sword fight.)*

> *(Their fighting strategies are identical – same moves, same sequences.)*

HOOK. Don't fool yourself boy, you can't surprise me. I know every move before you make it.

PAN. I already have a shadow, Hook. I don't need another.

HOOK. Oh come now, Pan. I'm not your shadow, I'm your future. We can fight forever or we win *together*.

PETER. Have we met? I'm the one that never grows up and thinks you're evil. Neverland will *never* be yours.

HOOK. Never is such an unpleasant word.

> *(**PETER** and **HOOK** battle again. Flying, jumping, swords clanging.)*

> *(Wahoo!)*

> *(**HOOK** gains the upper hand again, **PETER** is losing.)*

To think you built this entire place just to forget that you're some abandoned little boy with no story of your own.

> (**HOOK** *wounds* **PAN** *badly in their fight. He's got all the power now.*)

Give in, Pan. And give the dream to me.

> (**PETER** *falters for a mere moment. Then...*)

WENDY & TIGER LILY. NOW, TINK! NOW!

> (**WENDY** *raises her magnifying glass in front of* **TINKERBELL** *who shines as bright as we've ever seen creating a laser-like beam of light. They point it at* **HOOK** *and he is blinded by it.*)

HOOK. Take that light off me! TAKE IT OFF.

PETER. That's perfect! Keep going!

TOOTLES. He can't see a thing!

HOOK. Whatever this magic is, it won't work.

WENDY. It's not magic, Hook. It's optical mechanics.

LOST BOYS, MICHAEL & JOHN. OPTICAL MECHANICS!

> (**HOOK** *hears the tick tock below.*)

HOOK. What is that noise. *WHAT IS THAT NOISE?*

MICHAEL. Like my mother said, "You cannot argue with a clock!"

TIGER LILY. I'd worry more about the teeth. You hungry, Jerome?

> (*Growl! Splash! Tick tock, tick tock!*)

HOOK. *Where is it? I can't see it!*

PETER. *But it can see you!*

>(**SMEE** *bursts in to save the* **CAPTAIN**.)

SMEE. I've got you, Captain! I'll save you!

>(**SMEE** *runs to the* **CAPTAIN** *and grabs him.*)

HOOK. *DO NOT TOUCH ME.*

>(*And in one swipe,* **HOOK** *shoves* **SMEE** *overboard, without a care.*)

TINKERBELL. Wendy, I can't stay this bright for long!

>**SLIGHTLY.** What do we do?!

>>**CURLY & TOOTLES.** Save us, Peter!

PETER. No one saves the day alone. We can solve this together. Lost Boys, Regular Boys, ideas?

MICHAEL. The sea glass, Wendy! Maybe it could magnify Tink as well?

WENDY. Yes, the seaglass in my bag! Very good, Michael! John, hurry.

>(*They run to Wendy's bag and hand out the glass orbs.*)

TIGER LILY. We don't need more glass, we need more LIGHT.

>(**TINKERBELL**'s *light has faded and* **HOOK** *can see again, grabbing a sword.*)

HOOK. You think LIGHT can beat MIGHT?!

TINKERBELL. I think there is no greater power than a lady with wings and a vendetta. COME AND GET 'EM, FAIRIES!

>(**TINKERBELL** *whistles and all her small* **FAIRY FRIENDS** *show up as balls of light!*)

WENDY. NIGHT LIGHTS BURN BRIGHT!

PETER, THE LOST BOYS, MICHAEL, JOHN, TIGER LILY & TINKERBELL. NIGHT LIGHTS BURN BRIGHT!

(Everyone takes the disks of seaglass and shines the **FAIRIES***' light through them, creating multiple beams of light all pointing at* **HOOK***'s face blinding him.)*

HOOK. AH! Stop this, this is not a fair fight!

CURLY. But it is a FAIRY FIGHT!

LOST BOYS, MICHAEL & JOHN. FAI-RY FIGHT! FAI-RY FIGHT! FAI-RY FIGHT!

(Cheers! It's working!)

*(***HOOK*** can't fight with the overwhelming light, he can't escape it.)*

(He flails his sword but can't hit anything. He steps back toward the lip of the ship.)

(He can't go anywhere but down now. He pleads...)

HOOK. Pan, you're nothing without me, *you'll never be the hero without someone to fight. PAN.*

PETER. *Never is such an unpleasant word.*

TIGER LILY. Surrender Hook.

HOOK. How can I? He made me this way. Every hero needs a villain.

TIGER LILY. Not every hero. *I'm* the hero too. And I don't need you at all.

(Then **MICHAEL** *steps up too! Then* **JOHN**, **WENDY**, **LOST BOYS**, *building steam!)*

MICHAEL. I'm the hero too. And I don't need you either.

JOHN. I'm the hero too, and I don't need you at all!

WENDY. I'm the hero too, and I don't need you at all!

CURLY. I'm the hero too,

TOOTLES. I'm the hero too –

SLIGHTLY. I'm the hero too, and we don't need you at all!

PETER & TIGER LILY. Tick tock, Hook.

(**TIGER LILY** *stomps the plank and startles* **HOOK** *who gasps and falls into the water.*)

(*OR.*)

(**TIGER LILY** *glares at* **HOOK** *who glares, realizes it's over, and jumps overboard himself.*)

(*The sound of the* **CROCODILE** *dragging him under.*)

JOHN. Did we...win?

PETER. I think we did.

TOOTLES. Which means that Neverland is free again!

LOST BOYS. Neverland is free!

PETER. (*Re:* **TIGER LILY**.) It's whatever she wants it to be.

(*Suddenly all of Neverland begins to change all around them. A sound shift, the lights bend, tectonic plates shifting, the story is changing hands from* **PETER** *to* **TIGER LILY**.)

(*The* **LOST BOYS**, **TIGER LILY**, **TINKERBELL**, **WENDY**, **JOHN**, *and* **MICHAEL** *come together.*)

CURLY. What's happening?

SLIGHTLY. What's going on?

TIGER LILY. The dream –

TOOTLES. The story – It's changing!

WENDY. Because it's hers now.

TIGER LILY. Not just mine. No one saves the day alone. And Neverland is big enough for everyone's stories. *(Pause.)* ButSureI'llGoFirst.

> *(Perhaps we start to hear the music of* **TIGER LILY***'s people.*)*

> *(***TIGER LILY***'s family is coming back.)*

> *(***WENDY** *turns to* **TIGER LILY***.)*

WENDY. You are the strongest, most clever girl I've ever met.

TIGER LILY. You too. Night lights, burn bright!

WENDY. Night lights, burn bright.

MICHAEL. Mr. Pan? You're welcome to come with us if you like.

WENDY. Yes Peter…are you sure you won't come?

PETER. Are you sure you can't stay?

> *(But they both know they can't.)*

WENDY. I…I'm sure.

> *(It's hard for her but…she's ready.)*

Come on boys.

---

* A license to produce *Peter Pan and Wendy* does not include a performance license for any third-party or copyrighted music. Licensees should create an original composition or use music in the public domain. For further information, please see the Music and Third-Party Materials Use Note on page iii.

MICHAEL.	JOHN.	CURLY.	TOOTLES.	SLIGHTLY.
Bye Peter.	Goodbye then.	See ya, Pan.	**Tootles again.**	Thanks for the fun.

> (**WENDY** *smiles and walks away –*)

PETER. WENDY.

> (**PETER** *runs to her and hugs her. This shocks them both. Neither knows what it means...but they of course do.*)

PETER. Goodbye. For now.

WENDY. Goodbye...for now.

> (*Then* **WENDY, MICHAEL, JOHN** *and the* **LOST BOYS** *exit with tiny* **TINKERBELL'S BALL OF LIGHT** *following them.* **PETER** *and* **TIGER LILY** *are left.*)

PETER. Do you think you might need a boy that flies and never grows up in your new Neverland?

TIGER LILY. I'll think about it.

PETER. I mean I can help with the mermaids. I think they come with the place.

TIGER LILY. They can't just keep grabbing people.

PETER. I know what is with that?

TIGER LILY. Is it boredom? Are they bored underwater?

PETER. I can talk to them.

TIGER LILY. Ugh, yes, you can stay. But you're on mermaid duty.

PETER. Deal. And...thank you.

> (**PETER** *and* **TIGER LILY** *do their handshake but this time they make contact. Laugh.*)

*(**PETER** thinks of **WENDY**... He looks back to where they left.)*

TIGER LILY. Go. Just go.

*(**PETER** hesitates. Then flies...)*

*(**TIGER LILY** stands tall, in charge, on her own.)*

Scene Two

The Nursery

*(**WENDY, MICHAEL, JOHN** arrive in the nursery.)*

(It's just as they left it. They call out.)

WENDY. Mother? Nana? We're back, we've returned!

JOHN. I made some questionable choices, Father, but I have renounced my pirate ways!

MICHAEL. We missed you and also we'd like some milk and a bit of chocolate if that's possible?

WENDY. Mother?

JOHN. Hello?

MICHAEL. Where are they, Wendy?

  WENDY. I don't know.

    JOHN. How long have we been gone?

      MICHAEL. Days?

        JOHN. Months?!

          MICHAEL. Have they left us forever?

            JOHN. *Oh my word, We've been abandoned!*

*(**MRS. DARLING** enters in the same lovely gown we last saw her in.)*

MRS. DARLING. My goodness, children, it's nearly midnight what are you all doing up and about?

WENDY.	**MICHAEL.**	**JOHN.**
Mother!	You're here!	***I am not a pirate!***

(**JOHN** *and* **MICHAEL** *run at* **MRS. DARLING** *and hug her.*)

MRS. DARLING. What on earth is this? I've just been gone the evening.

MICHAEL. So have we! But with swords! And crocodiles! And we almost died on numerous occasions.

MRS. DARLING. *What?*

WENDY. *(Muffling* **MICHAEL**.*)* No! Nothing. It was nothing. Just a dream.

MRS. DARLING. This is what happens when Nana isn't with you I see.

(**NANA** *barks from somewhere.*)

Into bed, you silly creatures. All of you.

JOHN.	**MICHAEL**.
Yes Mother.	Yes Mother. I'm awfully tired.

MRS. DARLING. That's the very first time I've heard that from you.

(**JOHN** *drops his sword on the way to bed.*)

Your sword John. Don't you want it?

JOHN. No I do not.

(*With* **MICHAEL** *and* **JOHN** *already in bed and asleep in seconds...that leaves* **MRS. DARLING** *and* **WENDY**.)

MRS. DARLING. My sweet Wendy. You know I thought all evening of you.

WENDY. Of me? Why?

MRS. DARLING. I don't want you to be sad about your future. I have every confidence that it will be an extraordinary one. Because you are not wrong. The world is changing, little by little, and it takes certain exceptional people to keep it changing. Which just might be you.

WENDY. What are you saying? Am I going to finishing school?

MRS. DARLING. I'm going to talk to your father about it.

WENDY. Really? Mother!

MRS. DARLING. But it'll take quite a lot of talking I imagine so don't get excited.

WENDY. Oh Mother, thank you. You see I've had the most wonderful and terrible and wonderful dream and I am now quite certain that I would be an excellent scientist...*and* mother. And adventurer. And governor.

MRS. DARLING. Please don't mention any of that to your father.

WENDY. I won't. Yet.

MRS. DARLING. *Wendy.*

WENDY. I have grand plans. You can't stop grand plans.

MRS. DARLING. Goodnight you rascals, you wildlings, you loves of my heart.

(**MR. DARLING** *enters quietly with* **NANA**, *just in time to say a quick goodnight.* **MRS. DARLING** *shushes him to not wake them.*)

MR. DARLING. Shall I tell them Nana is back inside? I don't want them to think their father is as cruel as that.

MRS. DARLING. All is forgiven if apologies are sincere.

(**MR. DARLING** *nods.* **MRS. DARLING** *nudges him or clears her throat like "that's your cue to apologize, dummy!"*)

MR. DARLING. Oh, yes. Of course. So sorry children! And Nana. And my beautiful wife.

MICHAEL.	**JOHN.**	**WENDY.**
Love you, Father.	Very good.	Thank you, Father.

MR. DARLING. And Wendy dear. Everyone at the party was talking about that Madame Curie you mentioned. Would you tell me more about her. In the morning?

WENDY. Of course Father. I'd like that very much.

MR. DARLING. Very good.

WENDY. And perhaps we could also discuss that finishing school –

MRS. DARLING. *(Cutting her off.)* Aaaaaaaand we're sleeping, we're quiet and we're sleeping.

(To the exhausted children.) Goodnight, my darling Darlings.

> *(And off they go again. Lights off. After a moment...)*

MICHAEL. I'm excited for you Wendy. I'm sure you'll get the *(Pronouncing it wrong.)* **Noble** prize one day.

WENDY. It's No*bel* Prize.

MICHAEL. That one too.

> *(**WENDY** smiles. A tap on the window and **WENDY** wakes and opens it.)*

> *(All of the **LOST BOYS** file in exhausted from their trip.)*

WENDY. Boys, you came! Look Michael! John, the Lost Boys have found us!

TOOTLES. So sorry we were late, Wendy.

CURLY. There's so many houses.

SLIGHTLY. But we made it!

WENDY. And I'm so glad you did. Come in, come in.

CURLY. Wooowww.

TOOTLES. This is your house?

WENDY. Well this is our room, in our house.

SLIGHTLY. *You mean there are other rooms in this house?*

WENDY. Indeed and we'll go over all of it in the morning. Now everyone find a pillow and blanket and settle in for the night.

JOHN. Shall we not tell Mother that she suddenly has a few more children?

WENDY. I think we can wait till morning.

>   *(As all of the **LOST BOYS** snuggle up and chitter chatter...)*

MICHAEL. Will you tell us one story, Wendy?

JOHN. One with a very happy ending if you don't mind?

WENDY. Of course. Let's have one story before bed. Just one though.

SLIGHTLY.	**TOOTLES.**	**CURLY.**
Yes please!	A very happy one!	I would prefer ten stories but I'll take one.

WENDY. Alright, alright, alright, Once upon a time, there was a very real place in the stars where dreamers could always go for an adventure...and it was called Neverland.

CURLY. Ohhh I think I've heard this one before.

*(The **BOYS** agree that this story will be a good one.)*

*(We pivot to... Outside the Darling house. Where **PETER** sits on the window ledge, listening in. On the outside, alone, but he thinks that's what he wants.)*

*(A street lamp outside causes **PETER'S SHADOW** to be thrown against the wall of the house. **TINKERBELL'S BALL OF LIGHT** appears too. After savoring the sounds of the Darling House...)*

PETER. *(To his **SHADOW** and **TINKERBELL**.)* What do you think? Should we...go in?

*(The **SHADOW** thinks...then makes a "let's go back to Neverland" gesture. **TINKERBELL** jingles disapproval.)*

You're probably right.

(Not wanting to go.) But perhaps we could stay just for the rest of the story?

*(The **SHADOW** and **TINKERBELL** approve and they hear one snippet of **WENDY**'s story...)*

WENDY. *(From inside the house.)* And he was brave and wild and – a good friend. And his name was...Peter Pan.

*(**PETER** smiles.)*

Milton Keynes UK
Ingram Content Group UK Ltd.
UKHW020116050824
446426UK00014B/358

9 780573 710872